The Ruin of Everything

The Ruin of Everything

LARA STAPLETON

Paloma Press
2021

ISBN: 9781734496550

Library of Congress Control Number: 2021932139

Book Design: C. Sophia Ibardaloza

Cover Art: Dr. Nanette Corda Catigbe

PALOMA PRESS
San Mateo & Morgan Hill, California
Publishing Poetry + Prose since 2016
www.palomapress.net

Table of Contents

Alpha Male   11

Intention Neglect   27

New   51

The Glory of   63

The Other Realm   71

Godspeed   79

Arrhythmia   87

Until it Comes to You   99

Flesh and Blood   113

Acknowledgements   123

About the Author   125

Para sa aking mga barkada, the Fil-Am intelligentsia,
for your joyous wit, your agile manipulations of form,
and your expressions of love, both cunning and as natural as breath,
as Rumi taught.

"We are a race of bastards, sinners and lovers, half-brothers."
Filhos do Carnaval

The Alpha Male

He was conceived of the one wild beatnik summer of his mother's youth. His father was a foreigner who worked in the kitchen. She was earning a little extra school money as a waitress. The father well understood the nature of the affair, and so, as soon as he was informed, he disappeared so that no mutual acquaintance could find him. Having the baby was an act of defiance by which she proved she was morally superior. Her parents disapproved, but she was, after all, their little princess.

How she saw herself: one for whom her adorers would do anything. And so she collected such adorers in her life. There she was, storming out in righteous anger and there they were, following, supplicant, arms spread.

She left the city and went back home. It was a small, wealthy, suburban town on the East Coast, where the obvious was better left unsaid. She married four years later, to a man who had slavishly loved her since high school. They believed in right and good things, which she determined and explained to her husband, and so, there were two things going on: there was their defiant love of the first bastard child. The stepfather made a point of demonstrating that he loved the first like his own. The mother held him just a bit closer in public as onlookers studied the half-brother, that *je-ne-sais-quois* about the features, his darkness. There was their right and good defiant love which manifested in their proud jaws at all public gatherings, in moments of pulling him closer at all events of the extended family: holidays, picnics. And then, there was their real embarrassment which was never given name but could not be hidden, the ever-present unspoken.

The mother, she did love her husband. As far as we can determine, it was a love of gratitude— for his tolerance of her tyranny, her demands and ridiculous temper. She knew it was difficult. But, we may also consider the other possibilities— sometimes, sometimes these dictators have a passion which runs as deep as the more obvious lover. They simply recoil from the expression of it. They find this expression degrading. And the mother, she did love her husband, in a way of which we can never be sure, and there was Tommy, the living evidence of her errant ways, of her betrayal, cuckoldry— and every woman on God's green earth, nun, and harlot and free spirit alike, was taught the fear of looking promiscuous. The stepfather, all his embraces could not erase the more subtle and profound work of his eyes.

And so, Tommy was raised with a self-conscious feeling of specialness and a feeling of total rejection. There were moments, moments unstudied, when they were washed to their essence, at the end of a long day, weary, doing what was to be done, as anyone does, forks scraping, chewing perfunctorily, and he could feel an unnamable emotion, radiating from the other four into him. It was intensely hot and cold at once, and he felt he was supposed to do something about it and if he thought long and hard he could figure out what. He did think long and hard. It never came to him.

His younger brother and sister, two years apart, looking like twins, naturally gravitated in together. If the mother saw herself as one leading and adored, then Tommy saw himself as hovering and waiting. He knew himself to be looking on as the others grouped off. And so, as the mother had taken her place, gone to school and took the leadership over other girls, walked in front of them, the son went to school and stood hunched over his books and watched. He leaned against a swing set post and watched. At the very heart of who he was: loneliness in the midst of people. No real connection. No real trust in affection.

From television, he learned that he would be tall, dark, and handsome. That he would be slightly devilish and sexy, and that if anyone ever gave him anything it would be fragile and beautiful women.

And so, at some point, as soon as the worst of the awkward years were over, he learned a simple psychological principle. He learned the high shuddering grace of seduction. The simple and obvious and vast and inconceivable knowledge of human nature. He knew he had a right to know. He presented his attention to a girl. He held her eyes a bit too long. He said he liked her shirt. And then he let them laugh, as girls do. He let them giggle in conspiracy, and then he withdrew his attention and waited for a sign.

It worked. And one after the other the school's most exquisite dolls relinquished their virginity, because they didn't just like him but loved him, which he never believed. He'd made himself of the movies. He was dashing, and they'd never met anyone who acted so unselfconsciously, so thoroughly out of dreams.

For this he earned the wrath of his school's male population. He wasn't an athlete, didn't travel among any of the other alpha males of their little world, and he did better than them. He didn't travel with anyone but the girl he was seeing at the time and there was always a next one. He had stolen more than one girl. It was his mark on the world. He got his ass kicked a few times, and from this he learned to watch carefully, be even more shrewd and strategic. He learned that if he looked insane, he scared people. It had to be a convincing look of insanity. He had to give in to panic and let onlookers see. It wasn't a performance, but a relinquishment.

There was a little strawberry blonde who meant something special to him. She was the one who remained in his mind. Her name was Phoebe. She was quieter than the rest. Once and a while, she would say something that he felt he knew all along. She would reflect and say something. He wanted to impress her. She was studious. He found himself working harder in school. He nearly four-pointed that semester.

And yet, he behaved little differently with her than he did with the rest, with this one important distinction: he never had sex with her, never even tried. He did, however, follow his ritual once he'd set his eyes on her. He sat next to her one day and then didn't for two. He waited to catch her searching the room for him. We can't hide our searchings, our eyes. And then he sat there again. He knew she didn't trust him. He knew she felt above the banalities of high school and so he learned a thing or two about poetry which she wouldn't necessarily know. He told her. He gave it time. She played the violin. She had integrity, and one day he kissed her lightly before orchestra rehearsal and watched her recede down the hall.

He felt something he had not felt before. For a moment, he felt an unfamiliar hope. And yet, he kept going in the same way he always had. He called Phoebe for a while and then he began calling someone else. He remained a better student, though, and began to develop an artistic snobbery. He read a few books.

He wouldn't have acted in high school. The high school productions were musicals and the athletes who detested him participated and the outnumbering would have proved humiliating. The idea occurred to him sophomore year in college.

Tommy hadn't fared as well in college. This was the 1980's, and feminism, still young, had passed on from its promiscuous phase. And then there was the AIDS crisis, and it just wasn't as easy for a young man to target and plot. Tommy began to feel he had been bad, that to be such a predator was bad.

And so, without his conquests, he was even more alone. He studied. He kept a journal. For some time, he had his first male friend, a short, long-haired, consummate egghead. It seemed this friend, Edward, remembered every name he ever came across, heard, read. He knew the names of all the philosophers of Europe and China. He knew the stories of the empires. He understood literary theory. He told the story of Rimbaud and read him in French. For some time, Tommy was made high by the consideration of Edward the Brainiac. He was honored to be considered his peer. And what Tommy gave back, Tommy who was afraid his most thrilling years were behind him, edified Edward's efforts with women. Tommy watched Edward's eyes and saw them land upon a girl in glasses. She was not quite so learned as Edward, but enough so to respect and appreciate such things. Okay, Tommy said, okay, give a little then go away. And it worked, and Edward loved Tommy. With Tommy's help, Edward would be the thinking woman's ladies' man.

Edward began to love Tommy oppressively. He studied less and popped by Tommy's room with joints and corny jokes. He made him tapes. At parties, he never left Tommy's elbow and so: Tommy, annoyed, claustrophobic, dumped him.

Tommy, without a friend to speak of and conquests few and far between, needed something to do. He began to act. At first he was really quite bad. In the beginning of the course, the instructor wanted to erase preconceived notions of acting, and so, he had them go up, one at a time, and read lines. Tommy was third. Okay, read the line. Tommy read it. No, said the instructor, you're "acting" and here, the rising star of 1971 off-Broadway theater, shook his hands in the air lazily and rolled his eyes. What does it say on the page? What is the first word?

"Please," Tommy said.

"Yes, go ahead now."

"Please…"

"No, you're *acting*." He used the same gesture, "What does it say on the page?"

"Please…"

"Yes, okay, go ahead…"

"Please, could…"

"No!"

They went on like this. What the teacher wanted, was inconceivable to Tommy. It was like staring at two identical objects, two blue pencils, two ticking, battery-operated, old-fashioned alarm clocks, and being asked: okay, which is the right one? Which? It was like some impossible loop in a stress dream. He took the experience with him. He couldn't forget it. It made him want what he wanted even more. He couldn't sleep. Food became bland, chewing a chore, women irrelevant etc. etc. etc.

And then, one more night on the edge of his bed, it came to him. Staring at the back of his hands, bleak and fearful, up rose a moment of clarity. It was like crawling up through the air vents, squeezing through the tin, lungs full of wet dust. He'd made his way. He didn't wretch. Up up up to the roof, to stand on the edge, on his toes, arms spread. Precarious was important, and thrilling. He crawled up into the dream. He knew, then, the difference between good enough and not, which is the difference between breath and breath.

He took out the play, "Please," he said aloud, "could."

After that, my friends, every moment was dedicated to knowing the difference. There he was, pausing with his head turned in the shower, that delicious hot water pouring down his chest. There he was with that look of intense concentration and discovery. The yes, yes. There he was on the bus, staring with recognition at a stranger limping up to the hospital.

He joined the Brecht Company. And his school, which had heretofore paid little attention to actors, this school, which had preferred the worship of rockstars, in bohemia, and athletes outside, began to buzz. It was the young women who brought the word about. The lovely young journalists who shifted their asses during Tommy's performance, resituated, put their fingers to their lips and went back telling the tale, first to each other and then in print. He was captivating. He knew how to get ugly, captivating in his ugliness, and soaring with adrenaline ten times the level of the other actors, who always looked a bit embarrassed when Tommy took his bow. He knew how to get ugly and there he was forty-five minutes later, beaming and beautiful, with that wild black hair *and je-ne-sais-quoi*s about the features. He no longer had to seduce anyone. They came to him. They plotted. They put much energy into making their way into his presence. He could tell when a student interview had little to do with the interview. He could sense when projects were designed for the possibility of his attention.

Soon enough, he grew bored. They were all too easily impressed.

He couldn't wait to get the fuck out of there. He picked New York over LA, as he saw himself as a man of integrity. (LA, its great wealth, would come later).

The first years were not so terribly difficult, as these things are for struggling actors. Even though he worked little, even though his skill counted for nothing and his exoticism made him difficult to cast, his twenty-second year was quite fun. He never forgot who he was for a second. And he waited tables, and he developed camaraderie with the people he worked with. He became part of the *group* which he had never had before in his life. Even when his fellow cast members had admired him, it hadn't been a taking in. Here, they were unified against common enemies: the customers, the management. He slept with the waitresses, one by one, and he wasn't the only one. Yes, feelings were hurt but they had to suck it up and keep going. There wasn't much time to complain. Tommy was relieved by the felling of the righteous indignation which had characterized his education. The restaurant staff was comfortably decadent. And what they did in the wee hours after a Monday night shift, was common knowledge by Tuesday at noon and then, they only winked and egged each other on. Tommy's powers were returned to him without guilt.

His career: he was cast as Mercutio more than once— a single scene in a ridiculously bad artist showcase directed by the girlfriend of Romeo. Of course, he stole the show but nobody came anyway. He did the same part in summer stock in the Hamptons, of that production he was quite proud. There, the actress of great repute and not fame played Lady Montague. She was the benevolent matriarch and she smiled at him as if she knew him. This gave him fuel. He was the special son. It all began to build.

Somehow the constant audition and rejection didn't faze Tommy, never made him question himself. He accepted rejection as the nature of the beast and kept going with a bit of glee and a bit of fuck you and no need to gather himself after a loss because he *knew*.

Eventually, he went to every call with a feeling of elation.

For others, luck was an astronomical part of the path of their lives. They might tell you it's talent, or hard work and concentration, but I don't much believe that. It entails work, oh yes, but it's much more a matter of pride, and secondly, I think, chance. They had to gather their pride for another audition, have the ability to look people in the eye with the certainty that they are good enough, the same way we bring about love. After all the no's, somehow, actors have to try and make the leap. The day after one good performance and a delicious triste, the right person might see an actor with charisma beating out of the chest. This is convincing. But how often does this happen? How often are the planets in alignment?

For Tommy, our Tommy, this happened nearly every time and soon enough things began to take off for him. He did a couple of rather embarrassing commercials, and then he did that independent film which broke him through. The director was a huge, beer-bellied man prone to ingratiation. He would have been easily dismissed by most anyone. He had ridiculously huge hands-- like sides of beef, they joked behind his back. His voice shook when he spoke, as if on the verge of tears and his eyes made quick darts off to corners like a horribly guilty child or a coke addict. When he had to make a decision, he screwed up his face in an expression better saved for private moments. He was pretty much roundly mocked by all involved, cast and crew alike, but Tommy believed in him.

Everyone believed once the film hit the festival circuit. Tommy's role was close enough to Mercutio. Next time he had the lead.

He moved to LA. He worked often. The world became one big playground of women, one big bordello, or better than that, he thought, full of the willing but less soiled. For some time, he wanted to see what he could get away with. There were many adventures. There was the time he took home the bartender and a customer and asked them to perform for him, together, to have them together and let him watch. The bartender was a lesbian and the other was not, and the way Tommy always tells the story, it was the bartender, who seemed willing from the start, it was she who stormed off in disgust when asked to kiss the other girl. Three women at once was his goal for quite some time. Not too young and vulnerable, experienced women but not too— yuppies of some kind, giving over to adventure. Women who had never done this kind of thing before, three close girlfriends. He was disappointed when one insisted on waiting until he was done with the other two. She suggested she make her entrance in the morning but he just woke up and left.

Within a year in LA he did his first ensemble film with a group of hotshot young actors, and for the second time he was part of the group. There they were with their magic lives and their drinking at night. There were four men and two women leads and so they were competing, which he loved. There was an attractive woman in costume, but she was a consolation. Tommy was sure he understood human nature better than the others. He let the others make their mistakes, but expressed his interest. He had to be missed just a bit more, be more sure. If he was in a conversation floret, and Paulette, (who was the most popular, for her wit and her confidence), didn't give him more attention than the others, he walked away. He often let her catch him watching her. Paulette was his first long-term girlfriend. By long-term, I mean eight months. She had red hair at the time, although she was blond soon after. She was tall and very, very slim. She was known for her deep voice, like a woman after a lifetime of smoking or of another era. Every step of hers, from bed to bath, from refrigerator to stove, was a strut. They hadn't played opposite each other, although they had both played villains who pined for the heroes, and worked in tandem in certain moments. Tommy's character was a drug dealer and a cad. Hers was a seductress.

As the film was released, they were all listed as the next big thing. They were the ones to watch out for. They were featured in *People*. They were the _____ of *Us*. An interview with Tommy made it popular knowledge that he was an insatiable reader. They called him a Renaissance man, it became part of all of his publicity and he was very squeamish about this because he knew it wasn't true. A UCLA graduate student cornered him at a club, started dropping names until Tommy felt very hot and cold at once, felt he should do something he could not place his finger on. Tommy excused himself. He looked back at the graduate student's face and saw a feeling of triumph.

His first long-term relationship ended without much notice. They were both working a lot, far apart, and when it was over, Tommy noticed he hadn't really cared at all. During this time, he began to make an astronomical amount of money. Against all predictions he did romantic comedies. Most of them were pretty bad, but he had such impeccable timing, such glorious unquestionable skills, that he carried these films, made them worth seeing. He did some action films and brought them the same qualities.

Every once and a while, he lucked upon something he believed in. There was the film adaptation of the British playwright's work he'd read in college. There was the quiet and profound story of a man whose wife was going insane. He was very good at longing, and panic, and shame. Even when he had to fight like a super hero, he brought a bit of panic to the fight, even when the director asked him not to do so. What he would do, would be to exaggerate badly the quality he knew the director wouldn't want, and then remove it by halves, with the principle of half-life until he had the effect he'd wanted in the first place.

Just a few of the inconceivable rewards of astronomical fame: he took a yacht trip to the keys with a favorite maverick author. He never had to wait *anywhere*. Every few months he made a family of the cast on location. There was almost always someone to unify with against common enemies. If the director was an asshole, at least he could laugh with his fellow actors about that. He loved his work. He couldn't believe the good fortune to make his life doing what he loved. As he got older and worked with married people, he learned who was faithful and who was not, made it his goal to convert the scrupulous with gradually less subtle touches. He almost always got the girl. He was wooed with gifts by strangers— carvings from Bali and Macao, guns, state of the art technology, rare chocolates, watches and things smuggled out of third world countries at tremendous risk. The most macho of men deferred to him, and he found, that the slightest of affection— if he were to play a fireman, say, and spent a day at the station house, and make one joke with one working man, he could light up a life. He could make a friend to reify any quality he wanted, as long as their fame wasn't equal to his, most anyone would be honored by his attention. He made friends of: musicians and maverick writers and even a pimp (for the sensation of street cred). European experimental directors and conceptual artists (for the sensation of headiness). Upcoming comics (for the high that comes after laughing for hours). All he had to do was show up at the door and say will you tell Mr. So and So I'm here to see him, and I enjoyed etc... Someone: cleaned his toilet, his pool, drove his car, cooked his meals, rubbed his back, made his phone calls, decorated his house. The effects of his fame were far reaching. A tiny piece of Tommy was worth grappling over. He overheard a guy he'd had in psych class in '84 bragging, a guy who now held a walkie talkie and worked in transportation— as if to have seen his face twice a week for fourteen weeks, in the prior decade, was an object for bartering. And the truth is, the truth is, Tommy's brother tried to get the info out as soon as he met a woman, because he saw them shift as the possibility arose. He saw himself reconfigured in their eyes: if you're with me, perhaps once a year we'll go to Hollywood. Maybe we'll go to Cannes. And Tommy's brother knew Tommy had everything to do with his marriage to the laughing slender princess he had.

Tommy knew that eventually he would meet Iris. He had always supposed it would be at a party. He never dared to dream he would work with her, be taken away for seventeen weeks, be locked up nearly-alone with her to allow for his ritual of comings and goings. As a matter of fact, the year he won the Oscar for best supporting actor, he had been heading toward her anyway. He had heard a story about Iris which had involved person X, and he knew a friend of person X and he'd been having lunch with the friend. He was going to throw a party.

He won the Oscar and if you thought he was cocky before, forget it. He knew he had a right to Iris, and they were sent off together to a tropical locale.

Like Tommy, Iris' story was trying but not wholly tragic, nothing worth whining over, nothing too worthy of our sympathy. At the age of nine, a girl of her clique was sent to inform Iris that she needed a bra. This was the announcement of her ousting. Until this time, she had been a fortunate member of the sweet and gleaming and cruel club, the club of pretty and well-cared for angels. She developed early and immediately thereafter, completely innocent, developed a reputation as a slut. It took her a very long time for her to figure it out, after she'd taken up smoking and kept the company of the bad, who met in parking lots and arcades.

When she figured it out, she was twelve years old, 5'10, fully grown, and standing behind her father in line at the airport on the way home from a too-long vacation. She was weary, and leaned over and placed her chin on her father's shoulder. Her father stroked her hair. Her eyes fell shut for a moment, and when she opened them, she saw a couple seated, facing the check-in line. They were in their thirties, which was ancient and frightening to Iris, and they were staring at her intently. She looked around to contextualize them, and saw a college-aged young man looking at her as well. She knew that the young man's looking away meant more than if he'd kept watching. As the waiting went on, no matter what she did, slumped against her mother's shoulder, walking to the fountain, she looked up to see somebody watching her. When she got home, she looked very closely in the mirror. When she got back to school, she began to cultivate the skill of being watched.

She learned that bringing about the gaze had less to do with the specifics of what she did and more with the specifics of how she felt. She must, at all times, feel languid and very, very clean. She took a lot of hot baths. She watched movies, and would, in the middle of pre-algebra, drift off into the role of gangster moll, which entailed both a bracing and a vulnerability. She didn't have to dress much differently from her fellow classmates, who wore jeans and sweaters. She simply had to let her eyelids drop, think very hard about the nape of her neck, stretch, notice her muscles were cramped and needed stretching. She remembered sensations. She recalled them. She set specific goals: at first it was her frenzied and ashamed classmates whose attention she had to have. She knew when they got louder for her. Then, she, against all standards of good and right, sought the glance of grown men. The principal, her father's friend. It was absolutely unnerving and unmentionable.

Of course, she was pretty much despised. She set everyone on edge, except for girls who were a bit like her, but never, never as charged, and boys who were either sheepish or who knew good and early that they were bad. These people were willing to talk to her, even fight for her. She always had a protégée, a girl, less willful, who might chomp gum in the same way and curse as much. This protégée generally walked a pace or two behind. This was accomplished by Iris' sudden decisions. She would never alert her companion to an upcoming left, to a change in locations. She simply darted about on impulse, and only hung out with girls who would follow. She was amazed at how much the girls would follow.

The first boy to love her, I mean really, truly love her, as she understood, was a man. He was a part-time telemarketer and dope dealer. She was fourteen and he was ten years older. He was very ashamed, but he was sure he couldn't help himself. Did I mention she was overwhelmingly beautiful? She remembered the way he touched her and imagined it all day long. It brought lovely expressions to her face. She dumped him for a local rockstar, who was only seventeen. The rockstar was much admired by the girls in town. With him, she could live with their hatred.

After a year and a half of community college, she went to go visit a former protégée in Los Angeles. The friend was working as a receptionist at auto-mechanic to the stars. In Los Angeles, Iris noticed that no one hated her exhibitionism, that, as a matter of fact, it wasn't much compared to others, that it was successful enough, but not excessive, tasteful.

The rest is history. People who knew her back then would say that they were amazed at the elegance she came to have.

This was what Tommy wanted all along: Iris. He hadn't even known it, but it's true. His joy was manifold. He became very generous and loving. He felt sincere love for his fellow man. He smiled with love in the faces of all waiters and personal trainers and asshole directors. He became effusive with compliments. He inserted the phrase "you know what I like about you, _____" into a significantly higher percentage of his conversations. He meant these things sincerely. And Iris, Iris, Iris, was perfect, raging, kind. He could not have conceived of this. In all his years of acting, in all of his loves, in all the years of portraying intense and exalted loves, he had not known it could go this far. Sometimes, he just pulled the car over and cried.

It was seventeen months before the first split second of taking her for granted came. Tommy fucked the visiting best friend of the young starlet on location. She was half his age and two. He felt it was in good taste that he stayed away from his costar, but when he got back, he felt guilty, and loved Iris, if this is possible, even more intensely. What I mean by this, I guess, is without a trace of reason, without a trace of his former understanding of human nature. What happened was that he became insanely jealous. She left him.

Tommy's depression lasted three and a half years. It included violent rages, blithering episodes, drugs and alcohol, rehab, experiments with religion, and months in a remote village where no one could find him. Later, he decided he would marry someone simply beautiful, interesting enough, kind, worshipping and safe.

What I'm getting at here, is also the story of Andrew, whose story, like Tommy's and Iris', entails a melancholy childhood. And like, with the story of Tommy and Iris, it would be melodramatic of us, it would be downright silly of us, to feel much pity at all.

With Andrew, it was his slightness. With Andrew, the problem was, that he was built fragilely like his mother's side, and not big and brutish like his father's, and so he was no kind of athlete. And so, athletics embarrassed him, gym class, his father's lessons in batting, horrified him and he began to shake and was pathetic. And so, his father was disgusted. And so, his father, whose greatest days were his young athletic days, could not begin to understand. The brother, through the fascinating caprices of genetics, was at least tall, although he was thin, and so he played a mean game of basketball. This wasn't their father's game, but after Andrew, it was certainly good enough. It was their table talk, as their father sat there, utensils in either fist, taking up space with his broad shoulders, big elbows, big chewing, there was talk of the practices, the games.

And so, inevitably, Andrew turned to books. Andrew was off to an ivy league school before it occurred to his father to notice, and then the father's pride was so intertwined with the shame he felt at not having noticed his son's great talents, that they repelled each other even more. And so it goes. He studied philosophy. He was very, very good at retaining information and associating ideas. Later, he became wondrously creative in his approaches. He developed a reputation.

And what does a man who is very good at what he does know he deserves? He deserves a woman who is learned enough to appreciate his efforts.

Andrew's search for love was frustrating. Initially, there was the problem of his slightness and physical self-consciousness. But like most wimps and harmless outsiders, just-a-bit outsiders, he came to measure himself in other ways and choose among people like himself. He had dated a few women who were proud of his mind, fellow academics all. The problem was, that he wanted someone he respected, someone whose opinion counted, but he also could not help winning every argument, because he just argued so damn well. And so, the type of woman he chose— at least somewhat proud, could not take his quips and cunning references. Losing made him panic, and so the closer they came to making their points, the faster and louder he worked to put his debate together. One night, he followed Angeline around, as she capped her ears with her hands and sung to herself. He wanted her to concede a point about her favorite German philosopher. It was her German philosopher, but still he insisted. She said you have beaten and humiliated me. She said you win, goodbye.

After the second one left for the same reason, he became afraid of himself. He felt he had only one choice left— marry a woman who didn't mind losing, who somehow liked it— she'd have to be a bit masochistic and at the same time, the prospect very much depressed him.

He was thinking he should marry someone and hope for the best. What I'm getting at, is that, well, I think our greatest joys come from the things we never expected to have. Andrew never expected to find a woman he really and truly loved who could stand him, not an

24

uncommon problem. During this time, his publications were certainly brilliant and his teaching style openly hostile. The young hated him. His life was horrible. He was wretched. He felt this way for fourteen months. And then on a randomly better day, a day perhaps only better because of the sun, in which he was a bit more attractive, he met Phoebe, who played the violin and was a professor of ethnomusicology. She was very pretty with glasses. Her strategy: when he went off the handle, she smiled at him condescendingly. She once said: okay, you win the conversation. That was fun. Now let's have sex. She diffused his panic. His repulsive, unbearable, propensity to argue became an amusing quirk. She was the great gift of his life. And to think, he almost chose to marry without love. He was ecstatic. For a few years, he was kinder and his students enjoyed his classes.

And then what happened, was Tommy decided to marry someone simply beautiful, interesting enough, kind, sweet and safe, and he thought of his high school crush. Tommy googled Phoebe. He had coffee with her far away from Hollywood. He had just happened to be in town. He called six weeks later, at her office. He worked his way in.

For a hot second, she was resistant. She thought, not so much of Andrew, but of how foolish she would look to her colleagues, and then she thought, well, I'll never have to think of my colleagues again. The next time she saw Tommy— ahh, the rest is history. The voice. The voice. The tabloids barely mentioned it. Iris' life was much more interesting. Tommy kept these things very private. And Phoebe, she often felt invisible, but life was so thrilling it was a tradeoff well worth the while. She tolerated his philandering. She was almost unaware. Tommy, he had fun, excitement, a sense of accomplishment, and in a sense he loved his second wife. It should be known, however, that it took a lot of energy to look away from the bold, the blazing face of the wound, to keep his gaze always to the periphery. For the rest of his life, it took that energy. And Andrew— Andrew grew meaner and further hated by the young.

Intention Neglect

Violet's brother was a removed, cagey young man as long as she knew him, which was only sixteen years. Her mother had left him in the Philippines when she married a white man. He was two when she left him, eleven when she brought him over. He had an accent, and though Lansing, Michigan was equal parts Mexican, Black and white (the Vietnamese came later) and his foreignness and brownness were nothing new, he got beat up every other day because he feared getting beat. Sudden moves made him start and that made people want to hit him. Remember, the greasy kid in the back, who is getting beat up at home, is most likely to get beat at school as well. Unless the child is also entitled enough to become a bully (this counterintuitive combination is not so uncommon), the boy or girl will be humiliated by children and teachers alike. Teachers are more subtle, with sighs and glances and cruel notes on exercises.

The Autoboom was over and the fathers of many of these children were drinking and stomping around. The Union wasn't what it used to be: trickle down misery. They owned big houses, but they were in terrible disrepair. Such was Lansing, Michigan in the 1980s.

Maria Luna Valesky wasn't beating her son at home; she was just ignoring him because she was ashamed. She knew, deep down inside, why her son walked about in the world cowering with his hands up over his head. Antonio's grandfather was her father, after all, and he'd spent nine years with his grandparents. Add abandonment to the recipe of abuse and what do you get? A young man who can't stop moving and who is never moving forward. He is only ducking and not daring to dream. She never even looked at him. He never looked at anyone. She hardly said his name. He was the embodiment of all she'd ever done wrong, and what she'd done wrong was intolerable. Maria Luna never told herself any of this, but once and a while she thought of the hot little tin house near the base she'd been born to, the circumstances that made her choose between husband and son, and she cursed fate. She was the prettiest of three sisters, and she suspected that her parents (to whom she sent three hundred dollars a month) had planned such a thing all along, which is why they ran off Antonio's father. Her father ran him off with his wicked eyes and a broken bottle and a willingness to go mad with rage.

Mr. Valesky always resented the support of his wife's extended family, thought of the things they could have had— a better house, a new car instead of a beat up old one. The two worked hard and Antonio had his own room, which was more than she could ever have imagined in her own childhood. He had good shoes and a kind-enough stepfather who never looked him in the eye either. Mr. Valesky never hit his stepson, though Antonio never stopped believing he would.

Violet, who was seven when her brother arrived, the apple of her father's eye, kept her eyes averted as well. She knew the fact that she'd been chosen had something to do with the fact that her father was white. She was frightened of her brother and she didn't know why. He was the bogey man. As much as we fear the bogey man coming to get us, we also fear he'll bite us and we'll get it too.

Antonio came to believe himself wretched and alone.

In 1985, ambitious for her daughter, Maria Luna insisted they move one small city over to East Lansing, with its college-prep public school. Michigan State was the primary focus of the town and 90% of the students went on to college. It was too late for Antonio who ended up joining the navy (dreaming of sailing back to an aunt who had loved him unconditionally but also let him go). Violet, however, lonely amongst these foreign suburbanites, devoted herself to the task. Here, she developed the removal of long-term ambition. She studied. Will Valesky was resentful of being taken from his friends; he was uncomfortable waving at the graduate students who also lived in their apartment building. He was humiliated that Asian and African foreign students had more status than him, afraid they would steal his wife, but he loved his daughter and planned to go back one town over as soon as school was done.

Violet got into Brown, not only that, she had a scholarship. She wept with the knowledge that her life would be something she could never have previously imagined. She watched everything with wonder, green lawns, the sons of senators. She was frightened, and honored, one of the nation's chosen.

She wanted to do everything right. She sat in front with her pen upright, poised, wanted the professor to see her that way. She nodded at her favorite points, Jung, Machiavelli, Gertrude Stein and she noticed this drew the professors to her; they would start looking over, wanting her support. She wrote vocabulary in the corners of her notebook "bildungsroman," "synecdoche." She went out one night a week, just Saturdays, instead of two. This was her plot to excel. She wouldn't waste any time being drunk then hungover like the other, neglectful young people.

It was this resolve, this fear of falling off that helped to attract Violet's first boyfriend. He took it as hesitation and he wanted to win her. His name was Rigoberto de La Cruz, son of a wealthy, white, Mexican businessman. He was torn between being a great artist/political figure in the Latin American fashion, and being the king of Hollywood. Brown was a compromise with his father, he'd wanted to be in LA, but at least now, his English would be unquestionable; and he could later go to Hollywood if he wanted, at least know well his Homer and Moliere and Machiavelli if he chose to sit at a great desk in Mexico City and write verse. He appreciated that his father gave him such choices, as long as he really accomplished something.

He saw Violet in the computer center, in the early days of computer centers. He had expected to get himself a leggy blond, laughed when he saw there were hardly any at Brown, never thought he'd pick a girl like Violet. A girl, a *mestiza*, thick like a peasant, upon whom his family would silently frown. He'd expected a girl who could pull him into the center of things, a pretty, lean, WASPy intellectual who could introduce him to American Society (he hadn't imagined that "society" would mean so little on campus) as during the college years, well-educated American students generally prefer "cool."

But he was much lonelier than he expected. He couldn't quite articulate himself in English as well as he'd thought, he wanted to roll around in his own slang, and there she was looking as foreign as he felt.

She had a loose, thrown-up ponytail, and she was concentrating and she seemed distant, in her own world, and she had dignity in spite of her obvious lack of social position, like the girls who'd gone on scholarship to his elite high school. Not truly impoverished, but members of the unromantic lower middle class, daughters of single mothers (always), executive secretaries, and school teachers.

He went and sat next to her. He felt quite nervous doing it— though he'd been a very successful teenager with the ladies in his bohemian Mexico City. He'd learned that American women were quite unused to charm and he had no idea what to say to them. The girl, Violet, was unplaceable. All of these reasons to stay away, but he'd had no one to speak to and he had to change that.

"Hi," he said, a short, brown-skinned white man with blue eyes and a mane of gold-brown hair. Violet, couldn't imagine his motivation, and she was writing about Yeats. "Hi," she returned, and continued staring at her screen. Rigoberto, who had spent all the years of his high school education high on the attention of girls, who was charming and rich and could have what he wanted, found himself humiliatingly nervous and needy. He had been very lonely over the weekend, with no party to go to. He had written in his journal, "Maybe I should have tried to bring a friend." And then, "No. Quit feeling sorry for yourself. Nothing happens unless you make it happen. Who are you? Fix this."

"I am Rigoberto," he said. She told him her name, still very confused by this ritual she had not experienced before. "Violet?" he said, "Where are you from?"

"Michigan." For a moment, he felt ashamed of himself— would changing countries reduce him to selecting common girls? And then he felt ashamed of his bourgeois attitude. This is what the well-educated teenagers he'd known accused each other of in moments of conflict, the bourgeois attitude, though Rigoberto and his friends had had themselves enough maids and waitresses and had learned to quash their guilt.

And still, this girl was giving him nothing. He told her he thought she was Latin American. He said he was going to speak to her in Spanish. She felt flattered. "Latin American" sounded admirable to her, classy. She softened. He continued to ask questions, and though he was annoyed she didn't reciprocate, his pride was now involved in seeing this through. She sat squarely in front of her computer. He leaned over, with his elbow on the desk, leaning up to look in her face and when he asked her to dinner, she answered with a dull stare into the middle distance. "I guess we could do that."

Violet spent the first part of the evening racking her brain because she had some vague memory of having eaten in a restaurant with table cloths once before in her life and couldn't recall where it was. It was frustrating her. There were candles with gorgeous small bright flames, wriggling as Rigoberto spoke, a dark room, a roll in his hand. She found herself unsure of her manner of eating and so, she watched him and imitated. He cut things into small pieces, but then placed his fork in his mouth with exuberance and so she did the same. She stiffly raised her utensil in an arc.

The conversation was stilted enough that he almost gave up on the idea of sleeping with her. He had asked about her family. She didn't seem to want to talk about it, as if he were being invasive. She said her mother was a nurse (a lie; her mother was a nurse's aid). She had been tempted to say she was a doctor and somehow, after nourishing a more extreme lie, it felt like the truth. About her father, she said, "He had some stuff with… He had some stuff around management." She made no offer to contextualize, and she showed such clear discomfort, eyes dropped and to the left, that Rigoberto abandoned it, lest she call him "bourgeois."

He told her he wanted to make films and she leaned in a bit. He felt her coming toward him. "Wow," she said, "I love movies." She wondered if it was okay to say "movies" instead of "films," and it wasn't even true. She never watched movies. She had spent every spare moment studying.

There is this great Spanish filmmaker named Buñuel, he said. She nodded as if to say, I know, but when he asked her which films she'd seen she said she hadn't seen any. And so, he told her about *Belle du Jour* and its tone of erotic desperation.

This awkward situation with Violet confused and unnerved him. He had never been with a student before without having a vigorous conversation of ideas. This is what got a modern girl to put out. He had to say a couple of times, "You are right. That's true!" and make them feel he was a good listener. He couldn't figure out who she was. He had known scholarship girls. They were more argumentative than young women of his own ilk, they had something to prove. They liked to let him buy them things, then barely thank him. That's what Violet did. After dinner, she said, "thanks" as she was turning her head, so he wasn't quite sure she had said it.

On the walk home, he felt that if he only said the right thing, she would join in the effort, and of course, put out. He said she was very pretty and that she looked a well-known actress/singer. He said he'd like her to see Mexico. He asked her about the Philippines, to which she responded with shrugs and looks off. Near her dorm, he reached for her hand, which she allowed to sag loosely in his, like a super-feminine girl's handshake, though she was hardly superfeminine.

He kissed her under the front door light, right in front of the security guard and he had to stand up on his toes a bit as she was taller than him. He was moving a hand around the small of her back as she pulled away. They had a similarly excruciating second date, but he was wise enough to take her to a film.

On this second night, he kissed her on the sidewalk, further away from the eyes of security and he ran his hands around her without objection while she had that same superfeminine limpness. It felt very good to Violet, who was rather inexperienced and she decided to let him do what he wanted. She was tired of keeping her secret, her virginity, of laughing along as if she knew as the other girls talked about sex.

He didn't call for a while. He had to wait for a convenient date when his roommate would be out because for sure he had to have her on the third date or all of this would be for naught. He wasn't feeling very good. His grades were low because his grammar was off, and he was embarrassed by having to take his essays to a nerdy tutor, a superior-acting gringo. This tutor seemed to delight in changing infinitives and gerunds. "'We should stop to consider' means something very different," he scolded, "from 'we should stop considering.'" Was that a smirk?

He wasn't feeling good and he had to have Violet, and he got rid of his roommate, and it was terrible that she hadn't told him she was a virgin. What an odd omission— he didn't want to be that significant in her life, he was feeling guilty and she bled and then just lay there as he tried to cuddle her. They didn't even discuss it.

And so commenced their quiet, awkward relationship. He called her. They sat next to each other studying. She smiled weakly over at him as he looked at her with his watery blue eyes. He thought of things to say. He taught her a few words of Spanish. They waited for their roommates to leave. He asked her questions. Where did she see herself in ten years? What was she studying? Was 20th Century European History interesting today? Violet loved this; no one had ever sought to know such things about her before. The problem was, she didn't reciprocate. She worried she might be being invasive.

One night, she hung up the phone. Her roommate, a graceful young lady named Jessica from Boston, was hunched over her Philosophy of Science textbook with her fingers in her hair. Violet thought of the word, "love" and then she felt very ashamed and confused and frightened. She lay across her narrow bed, turned toward the wall, lest her roommate sense the enormity of her emotions and ask about them. Violet didn't answer Rigoberto's calls for a couple of days, thinking he might sense her desperation.

Things got even worse one day, after the day in American Lit, when Violet raised her hand. She was training herself to speak more in class. The professor had asked about the effect of Faulkner's long, winding sentences. "It makes everything happen at once," said Violet, who might have sounded angrily stern because she was nervous and trying to control her voice. "It's like he's saying, 'There's a professor in a brown skirt, and a kid in a blue hat and a pencil on the desk and the students are writing and the sky is a bit gray today.'" She was surprised by her own acute explanation, though she feared she went on a bit long and suddenly stopped.

As she finished, a young woman said from the back, "Synchronicity. It collapses time." Violet blushed. Why hadn't she thought of such efficient language? The other girl's voice was smooth and pleasant. The contrast hotly embarrassed Violet. She felt terrible that day, slightly sick. She carried an expression of disgust and hurt.

When she saw Rigoberto that night, in the library, she had used a bright brown lipliner that remained after her lipstick had come off with her dorm dinner. She had a brown-red outline around her mouth, and not only that, it was completely uneven, with an arc toward the outside on the left side and an arc toward the inside on the right. It made Rigoberto smirk and she thought he was laughing at her for a phenomenon related to the Faulkner incident. She recognized fear and shame, but she could not have explained that she was afraid and ashamed because he might have thought her vulgar. Violet only knew she felt she was doing things wrong. She seemed very angry as they studied silently. She pinched her little misshapen mouth down toward her textbook. Fearing she might reject him for sex that night, he suddenly remembered he had to get up early and left her at that intimate little table near the stacks.

Violet, on some level, had expected him to disappear all along, and so, when he didn't call for a couple of weeks she was hardly surprised. She was always on her way to the library anyway. She shouldn't be thinking a moment about this anyway, as she was going to read up a little extra on Faulkner. One day, on her way over the lovely winding sidewalk over the green, green grass, she saw him laughing next to a long lean blond with an asymmetrical haircut. She was almost relieved. She knew it had been a joke and she hated him for mocking her.

For the remainder of her years at Brown, Violet always had a boyfriend, the nerdiest most awkward *gringos* she could find, one after the other. There was Peter, the tall and thin son of a University of South Dakota philosophy professor with a toss of brown ringlets over his head. He always seemed to be crouching as if he had to use the bathroom and he felt like a failure because he hadn't gotten into Harvard. One day, he made a veiled comment about affirmative action— suggesting that his best friend in high school, the son of an African-American history professor, hadn't deserved to get into Yale. Violet was furious (she often felt questioned herself), but instead of arguing, she decided she would never have sex with him again and wait for him to break up with her, which he never did. When they separated for the summer, she quit taking his phone calls until her mother told her to do something about it. She promised she would, but she was working nights as her parents worked days and Maria Luna couldn't really force the issue. All Violet had to do was turn the ringer off all day. Finally, Mr. Valesky chewed him out, told him to take it like a man, and he never called again.

Sophomore year, she took up with Ted who had a bit more of a backbone than Peter. He was from the suburbs of Atlanta and was a twin. There was something about his hair, it was sticky as if he used excessive hairspray. He didn't seem to have any hairspray though, Violet even scoured his bathroom for it. His brother Tom, went to NYU, and Violet was shocked to see a photograph of the brother because he was much better looking than Ted though they were identical. He stood up straight and had a confident smile and a simple, flattering haircut that made their wide jaw look manly. Ted's hair stood up like a flame, like an accidental punk rocker, and it made his head look wide on a skinny neck. There was a photo of the two of them leaning against a car. They both wore jeans and a t-shirt but Ted's were too tight and short.

"Are you the youngest?" she asked, staring at the photograph on his night stand as he collected his books one night. It fascinated her that even five minutes might provide a birth-order dynamic in the family. Sometimes the youngest gets out of the way knowing the oldest is meant to take up space. And then sometimes those orders, as with Antonio and Violet, are broken by other more powerful forces.

"No," Ted said defensively, as if she'd accused him of doing something wrong. She decided her mother had "chosen" Joseph. And her suspicions were later confirmed when the frowning woman came to visit. She bragged about every simple thing that the younger twin did. He got an A- in chemistry, what a difficult course. He'd make a good surgeon. He brought me for the best Italian dinner and he'd learned to cook Eggs Florentine. "God, Ted," she said, "when will you learn a thing or two about politics?" She tested him on the names of cabinet members. To Violet, she said, "And what will you do this summer?" And Violet heard *what do your parents do?* And she said, "Medicine."

"Oh," said Ted's mom, "like Joseph."

The relationship ended because, well, mostly because Violet didn't want to have sex with Ted after about four months, but ostensibly because one day, sitting on a concrete bench over an expanse of lawn, the conversation wandered to what kind of bank account Violet had. Violet felt angry. She felt like he was going to judge her, like she better have the right kind of bank account. "None of your business," she said, which turned into an argument which turned into a breakup.

Violet approached her final college boyfriend, Alex, the day she broke up with Ted. He wasn't as literally physically nerdy as the others, but he had more social anxiety, was clearly, deathly, shy. She walked right up to him in English Modernism, a fifty-seat classroom, occupied by eighteen students, with plenty of empty chairs, and sat down next to him. It was so easy to pick up shy boys, and they were so easy to deal with, Violet didn't understand at all why the other girls didn't do it. They were together until they graduated. Violet strictly would only have sex with him once a week, eventually that was all he expected. He had very neat, long hair. His father was a lawyer in Omaha. They studied and ate together and never fought. He taught her to make chicken marsala. She told him the truth, that her mother was a nurse's aide. He had trouble speaking much at all, even after they'd been together for a year. She could feel the weight of him, sinking into the couch next to her at the Student Union, waiting for her to initiate things. Want to go home and eat? Sure. Want to eat falafel? Sure. Did you like the film? Yeah, sure. After a while she felt like he was dumping his responsibilities on her, like a limp, drunk, body she had to care for after the party. One reason they made it through graduation was because vacations separated them and there wasn't much talking to do on the phone.

Summer before senior year, Violet went home to wait tables at the same chain restaurant she always did. Antonio had a girlfriend. He lived up the road with a girl from Poland. He'd met her at a club in Detroit. The girl was so vulnerable, so plump and soft and helpless that Violet almost fell in love with her too. Her name was Dorotea, and she was a pale brown-eyed blonde. When Violet was friendly to her, said hello and shook her hand, she seemed downright grateful, smiling meekly, hungry for human company.

Dorotea was wondrously stacked. She struggled with her English, and just loved that the Valeskys—who knew little about their Eastern European ancestry beyond their great-grandfather, were willing to listen to her. One day, Violet took her to the bakery, and she asked, with that voice, childlike, sweet and guttural, "Thees is bread?" and then "What is your name?" meaning the bread. "Whole wheat" responded Violet, grinning and protective.

"I say to Antonio, em, er, we are go-eeng," she acted out whatever she said. "Go-eeng" was two fingers walking. Within a month, she improved astronomically.

The family was stunned. They hadn't realized Antonio was so special. He had come back from the navy with the same heaviness. Will resented his stepson even more then; he brought this inescapable morose feeling to their home. He ate is if he were wounded, holding his food in his mouth, forcing himself to chew and swallow. They had moved back to Lansing and Will and Maria Luna had had, until his stepson returned, a simple routine of dinner and TV. Maria Luna cooked and pampered her husband with questions about what condiments he'd prefer and compliments about how he was a good husband because he was funny. He liked to tell his wife stories about work and make her laugh. They called the secretary "Edna" behind her back though her name was Pam, because it fit her steely bouffant and black 60s glasses. The other Will had started to call him "Will Valsectami." That guy's a character, what can I tell ya? Mr. V had been very happy, living next door to friends, spraying the hose at those neighbors, bragging about his daughter who would one day be richer than all of them and laughing with his easy, appreciative wife.

And then there was Antonio back from the navy, moping at the corner of the table. Sitting in the extra chair as they watched the nightly sitcoms, never saying anything and pulling them down, day after day. He had begun to plan to tell Antonio to move out, maybe behind his wife's back because she'd never allow such a thing. He trusted his stepson's pride to protect him from her ever finding out. But then Antonio went to Detroit to visit a navy buddy where he met the Vulnerable Beauty at a club. He moved out within the month, up the street, close enough to make them watch in amazement and wonder what it was they hadn't seen.

Dorotea and Antonio loved each other. They leaned whispering against cars, ran every errand together— going to get a can of coffee or borrow a wrench or go to the gym. Dorotea stood habitually behind her boyfriend's shoulder shivering no matter the weather. If you ever caught her alone she had the frightened, wide-eyed look of an abandoned child, as if anyone could take advantage of her. Antonio had a new status in the family. He was still a figure of their shame, of the things they'd done wrong, but now he could not be ignored. Now they catered to him as if he were powerful, as if they'd be caught and punished for having betrayed him. Antonio looked happy. Even his stepfather made new gestures of affection. He tried to talk sports. Maria Luna asked him what he wanted to drink first: juice or soda, and then Dorotea and then everyone else. Will wasn't even jealous anymore. Antonio wasn't there every night, and when he came by twice a week, it was an event. When the young couple left, the house felt empty. Violet, that summer, began to dream that she would one day too have a relationship like her brother's.

On a July afternoon, Violet witnessed an interesting moment of jealousy between the lovers. She was walking up Saginaw and saw Antonio standing in front of Burger King talking to two Mexican girls. They struck Violet because one girl was as brown as she could possibly be, her skin was saturated with sun. This darker girl had burnt orange hair, the color of black hair dyed blond. The other girl was yellowish, like Violet herself, with black hair. They looked alike, not like sisters, but like the way best girlfriends pick someone like themselves to hang out with. They were both short with curvy figures and broad faces. They looked like different experiments in a paint by number set. Violet was walking toward them, planning to observe this to her brother to make him laugh. At this moment, as the girls were talking to Antonio, Dorotea walked out of Burger King with a bag in her hand. She walked toward her boyfriend to join the group. Violet observed that Antonio didn't break his conversation very soon to let his girlfriend in. He wanted to make her jealous. He left her standing behind a measure too long holding the bag and waiting. He didn't introduce them. He called out, "Bye Nanette. Bye Lisa!" as they walked away. Dorotea shook even more than usual and that was the one and only time Violet ever saw her mad. She confronted her boyfriend (Violet was in earshot now) saying, "Why you not introduce me two girls? So rude!" And Antonio stepped back, bemused. Aw come on now, don't act like this, he said, smiling, gestures larger than typical or necessary. They walked up the parking lot, parallel but further apart than usual. Violet had to run to catch them as they hadn't noticed her.

Violet felt herself becoming friends with her brother through the conduit of Dorotea. She was invited over to the young couple's house where they watched cable TV, or movies or *Saturday Night Live,* their quiet punctuated by Dorotea's questions. "What this means: "bunion?" or "outstanding?" or "dude?" She asked, "What is name when you are too sick and too hot?" she put her hand to her forehead.

In the fall, Violet went back to school with the feeling she wanted to love somebody. She was still with Alex, but she decided she wanted another type of guy, somebody more sought after and charming.

There was a pretty popular band on campus, the Pigmuffin's who had caused some controversy because a topless girl had come out to dance on stage with them, with only a string of pork meat covering her breasts. They answered criticism by also having a young man come out as well, with flank steak for a loin cloth. Violet decided she wanted somebody active, and glamorous, and so, she set her eyes on the drummer (who really was the shyest, most socially awkward member of the band, but still very different from her usual type). He was the Black-Jewish son of some divorced 70's hipsters, and he couldn't help but look like he was having sex as he played with winces under his small round glasses, and sudden thrusts forward.

She quit sleeping with Alex for about six weeks, deciding his nerdiness was an affront, the mark of a too-safe and protected childhood, which she envied. She wished he would eat more, and talk less about Bertolt Brecht and Marx and French Literary Theory. Twice, she brought over two bottles of wine and drank slowly herself so that he would be too drunk at bedtime to try for sex.

Meanwhile, she was plotting to gain the attention of the Pigmuffin drummer, Edward, who was in her Forms of Faust Seminar. He sat in back with his long skinny legs stretched forward. And his slept-in head full of hair, misshapen as a map, tilted rakishly off to the side. It was a wild crush. She decided he should notice her. She decided it should be gradual. She sat in the row in front of him two class days in a row, one Tuesday and one Thursday. On Thursday, just before class started, as they waited for always-rushing Professor Sinha to rush in importantly and write the names of some renowned authorities on the board, she turned around and looked Edward full in the face until he met her eyes. He quickly looked away. Then, using all of her strength, and dreaming of conversations of biracialism and rock and roll, she forced herself to sit on the other side for two weeks.

Meanwhile, Violet, made her first Filipina girlfriend, Annette Legarda, a short wide-eyed princess from Washington DC. She had as much wild wavy black hair as could fit on a head. She was a bossy older sister, and Violet didn't mind, because she knew so little of the Philippines save her mother's way of doing things, and wanted somebody to teach her what was her mother and what was the Motherland. One night they went dancing, and Annette walked about the room, and told people how to partner up. "You and Paul should dance because you're both tall," and Violet laughed inwardly because she was a tyrannical hostess, micromanaging the festivities and it felt familiar. Being part of Annette's crew, which included a superwitty gay Filipino young man from DC, and another superwitty gay Chinese young man from LA, made her feel hip and a part of something, even though she rarely spoke. They called her "Violate" and eventually she confessed her plans around Edward, and they called her "Mrs. Edward" and "Ms. Pigmuffin" and named their children "Pigletstarchproduct" and such things. They taught her Tagalog, she learned to count to ten and to curse and talk of sweaty body parts.

During the third week of the Pigmuffin drummer plot, she went and sat in front of the musician in class again. She wasn't answering Alex's calls now.

They were discussing the Great Chain of Being and she sat there, thinking he would notice and speak to her eventually if she kept looking up and smiling. He didn't. She sat there day two three and four and he didn't speak to her and then Annette called to say she'd seen him walking up the street holding hands with that waitress from Il Mare.

Something about this greatly humiliated Violet. She felt a large, arching, month-long wince, during which time she could not talk to Annette or Paolo or Mikey Tong. She felt they would know she was unworthy, that they were mocking her all this time as they made up nicknames and plotted seduction. She just wanted to study and she felt warm in Alex's arms.

The Christmas before graduation, Violet went home and Dorotea was gone and Antonio had moved back in with her parents. No one had mentioned this during their short, stilted phone calls: how are you are you studying enough are you resting what have you eaten how are the neighbors how was the party?

It was wind chill factor below zero in the Michigan winter, cold reddening the skin freezing mucous howling through their big, hollow, rotting rustbelt houses. Mr. Valesky darted ahead with his daughter's mangy old, plastic, 1970's suitcase (she suddenly noticed in the ride from the airport, she hadn't noticed how ugly it was before, how rotten and cheap) and there was Antonio on the porch, standing in the corner, drooling, with knees half-buckled. He awoke with the noise of his family returning, stood up straight, and fell asleep again into his bent knees, like resettling into a pillow. Mr. and Mrs. Valesky pretended he wasn't there. Violet had seen such a thing before only a couple of times, acquaintances from junior high, wandering the streets of their small gray town. And then in the movies, and then on a few weekends in New York.

They went into the house and Violet and her father sat down at the table. Violet's heart had never done such a thing to her, pounding pounding pounding pounding. Mrs. Valesky walked back outside with a thick old black coat over her arm, and then quickly returned without it.

They sat there. What Violet wanted most in the world was for nobody to say it, nobody say it make it not true make it not true and nobody said it and she noticed the VCR was missing and the Christmas presents were taken from a locked trunk and Antonio only walked through the room a couple of times on Christmas day and the presents and the jewelry went back into a locked trunk and her parents looked small and helpless. And she knew one day soon the trunk itself would go missing.

Violet went back to Providence and picked up an extra shift at work and studied and studied though her grades went down she sat there staring at her notes, her list of thinkers and concepts and she couldn't wrap her mind around the abstractions though she took the time to repeat things again and again, chanting on her walks to work. She always felt sleep-deprived. She felt her brain was permanently damaged. She didn't look at Annette and Paolo and Mikey Tong; she darted away from them and the rock drummer and she slept with Alex who one day finally said, "What's wrong with you you're so clumsy now and you don't remember anything I say."

"Look," she said, accusatory, "I *have* to work these fucking jobs and I'm tired." She wanted to righteously embarrass him.

After graduation, they moved to New York together, then broke up, living as roommates. Alex finally got himself a nicer girl and Violet didn't even seem to much care when he brought home that pixie-like performance poet in black cat glasses.

Violet worked waiting tables where everyone hated her because when they told jokes she looked at them like they were stupid. When they found out she'd gone to Brown they knew she felt superior. She sent her resume around to no avail (she had nothing on there save waitressing and her degree) and she kept working and working. She quashed her fears with labor and put money in the bank. Maria Luna was calling from Michigan, more than ever, asking about law school, hadn't she mentioned law school? Maria Luna was pleading, "Did you go off for four years to become a *servant*?" she hissed. Violet hated her mother for living through her so much. She hated such a burden, that her life had been lived in service to the poverty of her extended family. She had heard that Annette was working for MTV, she allowed herself to cry to the heavens that she wanted only to be young and happy and she didn't know how.

She began to wonder if all that work had meant nothing. In October, she got a job as an extended substitute teacher in the Bronx. It was terrible. It was more humiliating than anything she had so far been through. She was nervous, and it showed, and she was stuck in front of a math class and her degree was in English. She was teaching pre-algebra to a bunch of fifteen-year-olds, copying rotely from a text book, turning to the board more than necessary because looking out over the classroom made her cringe. There were thirty-three students at first, within weeks there were twenty. Only about seven ever seemed to listen. Every day she looked back to see Santi bopping to a song no one else could hear. "Santi, try to stay with me, please," she said with a true lack of authority in her voice. She heard Santi talk across the room about her ass. There was such chaos that she didn't know where to begin. Students in the back talked about sex and called out to each other. In the front, six girls and one boy sat attentively trying to follow the X + whatever. One of the girls was always drawing cartoons, but she seemed to absorb everything Violet said at the same time.

Violet wrestled with many different ways to think about the situation. She was afraid that if she asked for help they'd know how incompetent she was. So she ruled out calling in the principal. She told herself that the ones in front were the only ones that mattered anyway. She hated them then loved them. She left with a feeling of heaviness and woke (if she could sleep) with a feeling of dread. She didn't know she could mess anything up so bad.

There was a little bit of something she liked that she had never encountered before. They all asked about her ethnicity. They said she looked Puerto Rican or Mexican or Dominican or Colombian or Italian (meaning Sicilian like the movies) and she enjoyed the directness of the conversation. They seemed to take her as one of them once they found out her ethnicity, but it didn't help matters much, no one was listening.

One day Santi walked to the front of the room and grabbed the young cartoonist's notebook. Something broke and Violet was already a new person, how ridiculous she hadn't been this person all along. Violet walked to the back of the room simply took the notebook from his hand and returned it to its rightful owner. Santi seemed to like the attention. After that, she spoke to Santi through half the class "You with me Santi?" "Hey, Santi, why don't you race Bettina on number four bet you can't beat her." It was still chaotic, but it was a start.

In November, she asked Bettina why she always seemed to be looking at her so hard, with that stern, old-lady face like a weary token booth lady and Bettina started bawling and told her her troubles— two baby sisters and her mother sick. After that; Violet sought to know a bit about each student, she went systematically down her attendance book and she began to think one day she would have a handle on this.

Just before Christmas, miracle of miracles, they gave her an English class, and Violet decided she need only: step #1 know them, #2 earn their trust and then #3 prove their doubts wrong. And then she did.

She became such a very good teacher, so much so that she couldn't understand how other people didn't figure it out, couldn't do what she did, forgetting how bad she felt at first; it seemed so simple. She started by, on the first day, asking them to begin with anecdotes. She told her own story, about a drunk fake nun threatening to kick her ass. She said when they told their own anecdotes they could use "light" curse words like they use on TV, like "ass." "Bitch" could not be used unless one of the characters in the tale had actually used it. No "N" word. They spent half a class discussing "light" curse words, and joking about how to edit something so it wasn't corny. There was often a big joker in class. If she got the big joker on her side, she engaged the whole class.

Week two, Violet started to do grammar. She noticed that much of the class, except the seven studious in the front row, tuned out, started looking away or murmuring. She would stop and call everybody's name and make them turn their heads and look. When they started exercises, she walked around the room and looked over everyone's shoulder. She said something nice the first time she did it, hoping to inspire trust. The second time she went around the room to check grammar, she would repeat what she'd written on the board if necessary. People started to get it. After a couple of weeks, Damian was calling her over, "Yo, miss," to check and make sure he had full sentences and not fragments.

Violet was consumed. The only way to correct enough papers was to be completely sleep deprived, and then in order to both send money to her mother for her aunts, and make her student loan payments, she was waiting tables weekends. She wrote something nice on every single exercise, "nice image" or "funny" or "creative usage," so that students looked forward to getting them back and were willing to work on their grammar. She had them do metaphors and similes. They wrote "three example sentences" like "She is such a slob she leaves out, dirty tampons, three-day old cheese and marathon gym socks" (no you can't use condoms, tampons is bad enough). She brought in Shakespeare and they decoded line-by-line.

Violet felt a warmth, a tenderness in her heart that she'd never felt before. She realized for the first time that the real high comes from loving and not from being loved. When it was time to sleep, she felt safe enough to watch her own mind wander, was curious about what her dreams would bring. She felt a radiant hope.

In the middle of her second year, she met Vic the new gym teacher, who was a workaholic like herself because he was a social activist. He spent evenings at his local youth center, was into martial arts and was studying up on city politics thinking he'd get in the game. He was the son of Dominican immigrants; he'd been in the military and then to City College. She thought his face to be made of the most delicious combinations of angles and curves and golds and browns. He knew much more about politically conscious poetry than she did, pulled books off the shelf for her. Occasionally, they went to a poetry reading, though mostly they collapsed, exhausted, in each other's arms. She didn't talk much about the Philippines because she was embarrassed she knew so little though it gave her particular pleasure to notice Spanish words in what little Tagalog she knew— it connected her boyfriend and a worldwide experience.

Violet felt she'd found her place, and if only she could get her mother to stop pushing law school, she could live happily ever after. She found an excuse, the third year of her tenure at the high school, to skip Christmas in Michigan, and Vic took her to meet his grandparents in Santiago, Dominican Republic. The guilt over disappointing her mother that Christmas was one of the few things that made her feel terrible until Antonio died.

It took him four years of God knows what, sleeping wherever, robbing his own mother, vomiting in his own lap, to die of an overdose. There were only seven people at the funeral, the Valeskys, the priest, two neighbors and the navy buddy from Detroit who'd been with him when he met Dorotea. They asked Violet to speak about her brother and she said no. The priest blathered about abstract things: piety and the afterlife. No one knew how Antonio had been supporting his habit for years, where he slept on so many nights, who his company was. A stranger had found him on the stairs of a parking ramp. He weighed one hundred and seventeen pounds. God knows how many people had walked past him as he lay there, stinking.

During the Catholic ceremony, Violet couldn't lift her head to look at this strange priest making things up about her brother. She turned her head completely sideways to observe her father weeping. She had never before seen such expressions of pain. Will winced with his head bucking forward, his teeth and gums and mucous showing, like an animal. Violet was outside herself, watching. The navy buddy wept as well. He was Mexican and obviously spent all his free time at the gym, bulging, wide and short. He was leaning over sideways with his hand on his side like he'd been shot. He was so bulky, he could barely bend.

Maria Luna was stone-faced, except for a slight exaggeration in breath, her chest rising as if inhaling smoke. You never would have guessed she'd just met such tragedy. Violet realized she knew almost as little about her mother as she did Antonio. What she imagined of her mother's childhood, she'd gotten from a couple of TV documentaries on the Philippines. She imagined a blinding white sun and a sweaty wet heat and people walking up the road with wares on their head. She never met anyone else with her mother and brother's accent until she left Michigan; their mysterious language was both central to Violet's psyche and indecipherable. Violet knew the words for "How are you?" "hot" and "tasty" and most other simple adjectives and nouns and she could count to ten and knew the days of the week, all from what little conversation her mother and brother shared.

Suddenly, Violet's eyes began to stream so that her vision was blurred. She looked over at the watery form of her mother, blinking to see clearly, and was overcome with anger that her mother didn't seem to feel more. Violet's intense anger began in that moment and grew for years to come.

After the ceremony, with a longing against the laws of the universe, a prayer against the impossible, temporary belief in god and spirits, in the cold church basement full of folding chairs where the seven of them met to avoid each other's eyes, Violet approached the navy buddy. She had the instinct he might be the only one who really knew anything really about Antonio.

What she wanted to know: what happened to Dorotea? What kind of friends were they, Antonio and the Mexican man? Had Antonio had a nickname? Did he ever laugh? Why was this man allowed inside him when no one else was? Why couldn't he make himself happy? But mostly, mostly, she wanted to know if the friend believed Antonio had done it on purpose, if he really wanted to die.

Violet, of course, feared the answers to every single question on her mind, but she began anyway, standing before the squat stranger with a lukewarm coffee in her hand. She introduced herself, and he said, "You have a face-shape like Antonio," waving his hand over his face, suggesting the contours. And the man said his name was Eddie and she began, "Did you know Dorotea?" her eyes went blurry again, he was receding, the strange friend, and he began to sob and hugged her. He nodded, but Violet couldn't make herself ask more. She was afraid they'd run Dorotea off, that she'd seen the family and changed her mind and they'd destroyed his only chance at happiness. Violet wanted to ask where the Polish woman was, if she knew, but Eddie was clutching her, and then she didn't want to know. She wanted to know something about this man Eddie; they were friends, the only friend Antonio ever had. She wanted to hear something of his happiness. There had been something. "What did you call him?"

"What?" the man was clutching her and sobbing like a child. Why did he love Antonio so much? Why did he and Dorotea love Antonio so much? Why hadn't Violet?

"Did you call him Antonio in the navy?"

"Tony-O. We called him Tony-O."

Violet went back to New York with her anger and her question: had Antonio wanted to die?

On Monday, Violet rode the train into work. As the 6 train roared up she realized she would never be the same again, and that she was furious at something new altogether— the idiot defeatism of the poor.

She hated poor people. She hated the noise the threats to fight the bags under the eyes the malnutritioned boniness the obscene obesity the clothes that didn't fit. The not listening in class, the turning away away away. The shame walking into a bank, their fear and posturing. The yellowing walls, the peeling paint, the scotch taping of scrawled, misspelled signs. She walked to the school, past a liquor store with a spray of graffiti on the side. A huge black blob covered the beginning of a phrase, so it read, "rugs are the new slavery." She laughed and she felt hateful and she decided coming in to break up with Vic, who had been calling her parents' house all weekend, while she'd been saying she couldn't talk and she'd call back later. She hated her students, their big brown eyes looking up at her like she was supposed to make it better. She hated the world for the pressure.

She quit within two weeks, leaving her sprawled youth gasping. She temped quietly in the offices of arts organizations and women's magazines as she applied for law school. She waited tables on the weekend. She wondered if Antonio had purposely killed himself.

She was gonna own things, pricey earrings and a co-op in Brooklyn Heights. She would send her mother money, and she'd marry a white man, rich, and her kids would go to Andover and become important in the fate of the nation. All she had to do was spend every spare moment concentrating and be at the top of her class at NYU.

Violet was second year at the time of Sept. 11th. She lived in the East Village, paying half her income for a studio, and she was $85,000 in debt and it was only the beginning. Tuesday mornings, she didn't have to be on campus until noon. So, just before nine that morning, she was jogging at the East River park, enjoying the gleam of the gorgeous day, making sure she got enough oxygen in her brain so that she could sleep soundly, seven hours, and have a mind primed for absorption.

She was near the new amphitheater at the screech of the sky and as ten, twenty, two hundred million eyes turned toward the bottom of the city. She ran with others to stand on the overpass and watch the world turn into something where anything unspeakable could happen. The black smoke streamed off at an angle in that one section of the sky and from where they were twenty, no thirty, blocks away, they could see the bodies leaping from the buildings and all it meant was that Antonio was dead and he would always be dead for the rest of her life. White women with ponytails stood screaming in their little jogging suits and the buildings fell as they stood there in the gleaming blue and black day and Antonio was still and would forever be dead and there was no one to turn to.

Violet moved within months, three and a half years after his overdose then. She couldn't stay in the East Village because jogging on the East River now had something to do with Antonio and it had made her wonder, with profound pain, for a month, if he had killed himself on purpose until after that month of hard mental work, she was able to put it out of her mind, saying, I'll come to this again when I'm done with law school, when I've passed the bar.

And those days came and she went to the pretty cement benches at the East River Park, rebuilt as the neighborhood gentrified. She went to be alone and think and she sobbed for an hour and she still didn't know. And on her way back, she was walking behind a father and a son, Puerto Rican, the father was about thirty, the boy probably five, and the boy was on a bike. The father was walking behind the boy, his face scrunched up with annoyance, a short, thin man, and as they went over the top, with Violet a few paces behind them with her face wet and red (she didn't care, she had long ago given up caring about what people think, except to know she'd outdo them all) the boy made it over the top and started to roll awkwardly down the other side. The father said, "Use the breaks" and the boy kept rolling. "Use the breaks!" yelled the father, angry now, and the child was rolling straight toward the metal side of the ramp. Violet knew the child didn't know how to use the breaks and she wanted to run and grab the child and he rammed into the wall and he fell off, and the father ran to stand over the pile of bike and screaming boy and spat down, "I told you to use the breaks!" furious now with the boy's stupidity and Violet thought, passing them now, glancing down to see if he was bleeding (he wasn't) she thought, why didn't you just throw him into the wall? Why didn't you just pull your son by the wrist to the parking ramp and throw him into the wall with all your strength? You didn't even need a bike. She was yelling at the man in her mind as she made it over the other side. She was accustomed to anger and imagined yelling and she had the same epiphany she always had: *Antonio is dead and will be forever*, and then she had another epiphany and knew that it didn't make any difference if he had known, if he had admitted, he wanted to die or not, accident or intention, intention or neglect, it was the same damn thing.

New

I wondered if it was the light that muted our colors, if the sun didn't shine as brightly onto our streets, and that is why I couldn't get the same satisfaction in New York, my home.

In New Orleans, I had found myself experiencing little highs all day. I wandered around in that damn heat, looking at little houses and bushes and trees of flowers and feeling lifted when my eyes landed upon something especially bright or unique, some new combination of two or three colors, a main color with trim or some balance of secondaries of which I had not previously conceived. I was overwhelmed in moments or often just slightly elevated. I didn't know good feelings could be so simple. These are colors only designers know, or art school graduates or people who are quite good with such aesthetics because they love it and have made a hobby of decorating; I have not, but I will make my best guesses: teal, aqua blue, gray with a breath of violet, deep violet, midnight blue, soft green, powder blue, hot pink, orangish red, purplish red, deep red, indigo, shrill, pure yellow. I am from a very gray place, rusty Michigan, and in addition to the factories and strip malls of our childhood landscape, there are the overcast skies that make up the majority of the year. These bursts of color pulled at my heart. The sun radiated into me. I wanted to keep it.

One day, I stood in front of a little yellow shotgun with lavender doors. Magenta flowers burst from bushes on either side. I just stood there in the narrow street, wishing someone I love had been there to share it. Maybe that was it, the perfect amount of longing, that felt so good, that love with a twinge of sadness that something cannot be, no one else is there, or it cannot last forever. Too much longing is a terrible thing, but a touch of it is lovely. While I was standing there, with my mouth slightly open, I assume, a short, thin, very tan white man of about thirty came out of his house, and seeing my expression, smiled. "Do you want to see the court yard?" he asked. And I stood in that small space of wandering jews and bougainvillea. My head fell into my hands for a moment. What would you call that purple? I asked him. I guess that's like a maroon, he said, more brown than purple, brown with red. Yellow streaks wound through the dewy maroon and green leaves. And he asked me where I was from. And sometimes I say Michigan, and sometimes I say New York, where I've been twenty years, and this time I said New York, and he said, oh, I'm from New Jersey, and he said he had come down on a rescue mission after Katrina and decided to stay. It's so beautiful, I said. Thank you, I said. Thanks for showing me.

And I very much love New York, my home, and I returned with what I believed to be a new skill, the ability to *move* myself, just a little with color, like a minor version of experiencing a great poem or spectacular view or a scene in a novel or a film you want to share with someone you love. I returned believing I could bring joy to my life by noting the existence of beautiful colors. I'd read about this in the famous *Color Purple*, of course, many years ago: God wants you to recognize purple. After everything, there is still a beautiful color, and a character in *Beloved* too, an older woman who had been a slave just wanted to look at pretty colors until she died. I remembered these passages, but I didn't get it, really, until my month in New Orleans.

I knew I would seldom find it in a building in New York, just an occasional wayward restaurant or bodega, a random Queens hardware store, but I thought I could recreate it by looking at the lovely blouses of young women on the subway, their fabulous jackets, but so far I only have the same feelings for feet, ha! For our glorious sandals, a longing for a beautiful object that I wish I could freeze in time (ha! and now I sound a bit silly and shallow, if I have not already). What is it that is so beautiful about the curving heel with sparkles and bright feminine toes? The feet of New York's women are lavish in the summer, sparkly and arching, or flat and delicate with bold shining toenails against their whole-gamut range of flesh: yellow and blue black and pink and olive, cinnamon, and deep brown, rich and poor alike, sparkly Payless and sparkly Manolos. The girls, the ladies, the serious matriarchs of commerce, of academia, of city affairs, the secretaries and the nurses and the silly teenagers, sit on the subway, on their way to work, to the clubs, to dinners with boyfriends and girlfriends and spouses, home to their children, with their bright and lovely toes dangling off their lovely feet.

But I wanted more. I wanted the ability to see those colors all day, and feel simply lifted, and feel simple longing. And I sat down in an empanada shop in Lower Manhattan, painted blue and yellow. The trim was a bold baby blue, which did it for me, but the main color was a mustard yellow, and I thought it was dull, and I wondered if it were New York itself, the grayness of this city, or the muted sun, that would make a business owner choose the brownish mustard, over a high pure yellow. Perhaps it's just the bold Southern sun that gives you that feeling all day long, that makes every color look brighter.

Down in New Orleans, I had spent time with a guy just a bit older than me, the boyfriend of one of my Ft. Greene friends. She, Annette, had come down to visit, and Richard, her boyfriend and she and I all went to the Second Line together, and don't get me started on the Second Line. A hundred and ten degrees in the shade, and every last man plays an instrument, and a couple of women too, and there are two hundred people dancing in the street, on rooftops. And everyone knows the songs, and the teens don't seem to think it's corny. And what is this they dance? Something old, nothing I've seen on the street anywhere else or in clubs or videos or even old rock and roll movies. Like the images of Brazilians I'm most familiar with, they dance and walk at once. And people are selling hot sausages off the back of their trucks and beer out of grocery carts. And I'm happy just to be there and be there with friends.

And later, at the burger joint, Richard, who just moved down to New Orleans, tells us what it was like in Ft. Greene, Brooklyn, where I live, ten, twelve, fifteen years ago, that Spike Lee used to throw loft parties and Saul Williams would stop and chat with you on the street. Brooklyn Moon had open mics and the young people who hung there went on to make films and win Off-Broadway theater awards, star in HBO series, direct avant-garde legends and write novels that rip your heart out, books of poetry that young journal-keepers read here and there about the country. And it's over, he said. Ft. Greene is not what it used to be. And the Black bohemians who once peopled that neighborhood, have largely moved to

Bed-Stuy, and Bed-Stuy has not yet cohered into a center of culture and cafe hangs.

Richard painted a picture for me of this nineties Ft. Greene in which everyone was so young and beautiful, so promising, on the cusp, much better than the actual fulfillment, the break through to notoriety. It was over, dead, he said and I was a bit sullen that night feeling like New Orleans was not mine and I had no place to go back to.

But I am happier here, in New York. How do I explain that? I had little highs all day during my travels, but I often got lonely and felt uncentered. I missed my people. I came back a little bit friendlier, greeted with more enthusiasm, my twenty-years' worth of friends and acquaintances and I found it to be a wonderful summer full of parties and gatherings and nights in the neighborhood sitting at the sidewalk cafes. On the 4th of July, a Madiba regular, a guy from that the South African place in Ft. Greene, threw a rooftop party in Bed-Stuy. He had a huge roof, with a DJ and a raw bar: lobster and shrimp and oysters and two kinds of spicy steak and burgers and sausage and fancy side dishes like grilled beets and cassava. We didn't know Samuel, the wickedly charming Botswanan bartender could cook like that, like a chef, and there was liquor for miles, "I feel like somebody loves us," I said. Damn, I said, and Richard was saying Ft. Greene was dead. Fuck Richard, he's the one past his prime. And there was a funky, funky DJ, our friend DJ Weather, and I danced with people I had not danced with before, Juan C from Costa Rica and that young man who won Nigerian *Big Brother*, and everyone texted their friends and the party doubled then tripled before the vibe changed to something just a little bit out of control, and Victor, the Madiba regular who threw the party, started hanging in his own condo.

"Somebody should give Victor some," we were joking all night, and some of the heterosexual dudes even said they'd do it, and at the end Samuel told us, later, as we talked about it for a week after, he saw a woman pretending to fall asleep on his couch. A few of us at Madiba had fun imitating the act of arranging oneself on the couch in an attempt at seduction, Marilyn Monroe with your arm flung over your head and your hip arched out. It went on for weeks, the feeling of community that came out of that, the feeling that somebody loved us. It went on for weeks, the little stories about new couples and how people dance with this ridiculous elbow swing, or how many ladies Jaja (*Big Brother* Nigeria) rapped to and in what manner, and what the steak tasted like, with an exquisite equilibrium of various peppers and how much the whole thing actually must have cost and how Victor was a new man after that, how beloved and beaming with new choices of women. I myself called him Fancy Vic.

Victor had been coming around on the weekends at Madiba, when we drank our coffees after brunch or our Heinekens or Obama Mamas at night. I confided in the one particular friend I trust to tolerate my excessive nosiness: wonder if Victor is looking for a wife. And then I confided in that same friend who also tolerates my sappiness, that I felt like someone had given us each other for the summer. We'd gone somewhere special and come back a community.

New York is my home; I've been here nearly twenty years and I have my friends, close friends and party friends and run-into twice-a-year on the street friends. I have friends from my restaurant days, my bartending at the Nuyorican days, my quasi-academic life in the community colleges, my neighborhood, and because I am a mixed Filipino-Irish-American, I have the Filipino writers and intellectuals I gradually accumulated over the years. This is of great satisfaction to me. You can imagine my family was a bit isolated in Michigan, and here were these people who accepted me, and were even extremely cool about the fact that I am mixed and a very racially ambiguous person. And believe me, I have had many arguments about my ethnicity. People get upset about things they're not accustomed to. They resent the blurred boundaries, the threat to order.

People told me I wouldn't want to leave New Orleans, and they were right. I know my life belongs in New York, but I do think a couple of the happiest days of my life were down there. There was the day on the river drinking the most obscenely sweet hurricanes with Anthony, who was thirteen years younger than me. The hurricanes were beautiful like everything else, like the breeze off the water, and what would you say this color is? Flamingo pink, he said. Ahhh, yeah, that's it, flamingo pink. He was a poet, a young man with a journal, and he read books I know and quoted them and to have his attention for a moment made me feel like I was hovering at some pinnacle, like a piece of fruit that is about to turn, that must be had now. And amazingly, he knew a thing or two about scenes I had been a part of fifteen years before, the work of poets nearly a generation older than him, people about whom I knew stories of romance and personal squabbles and it was pretty amazing to have someone care about things I had been a part of. Anthony grew up in Ft. Greene where those writers of color I know lived in the mid-90s, then moved to New Orleans at the age of thirteen, and so, here we were with private understandings of each other, drinking flamingo pink drinks on the river. I told him I thought strippers in New Orleans were, um, unique to the profession, out of shape with bad teeth. Some of them got bullet wounds, he added, and by nightfall we were drunk enough to go test our hypothesis on Bourbon Street in one strip club after another. Anthony wanted to be at the Black club, Little Darlings, and when we got there, the girl with the best body, tall and thin-yet-stacked introduced herself to us as Supermodel. And later we laughed and when we got in bed we quoted writers we both literally and figuratively knew.

It was hot quick romance, and as it should have been, wicked and sweet. It was much better to end with my leaving, rather than to have the fact of the age difference bring on the end, to know he would soon enough grow tired of my advice and want to relax with a girl who acted just a bit less like an older sister or, gasp, motherly.

When I got back to New York, people asked me about Katrina. The truth is, I only saw a bit of the scarred remains, the houses with the dates painted to the left of the door, the water lines at neck level, small buildings with the entire back ripped off, furniture and scrap metal long ago removed. Although there was little evidence of daily life remaining, the room divisions, the walls down the middle left an impression of vulnerability, nakedness, roof blown off a life. Of course these images were nothing compared to the footage we saw on CNN during and for months after the hurricane. There were no longer cars upside down on houses, grandmothers lying in kiddy pools pulled on by the young and strong. No more young men on rooftops, fading in the heat, stumbling sideways on the shingles in their dehydration, obese women hunched over in crippling pain, pulled on by healthier relatives, sitting on anything that could float, plastic bins, two tied-together tires. The morbidly dying at the side of the road, babies howling outside the Convention Center, even Anderson Cooper, growing enraged as the days and the heat go on and the bodies bloat outside the Superdome, at the edge of the highway. No daily legends of terror, gang rapists and vigilantes. No miles and miles and miles of trash, soft, useless wood, boxes of clothes and family albums and teenage journals full of melodrama and bank records and grandmother's chair in front of what-used-to-be houses, and the filthy water, the infamous stench, the swimming in sewage, our own shit, a woman's, a man's face in their own shit, in everyone else's in human filth that daily humiliation modern life allows us to deny. Humiliation. Yes, these 2009 remnants of the flood were such tiny shadows of those contemporaneous images, that to be frank, Katrina wasn't much on my mind.

And so, it was a couple of hours later when I felt like a fool: an older man at the bus stop had said he had good days and he had great days and that he had decided four years ago that was how it was going to be, and that most people were good people, and I didn't do the math of the four years until I was on that same bus route back.

One day, as I was walking toward the Mardi Gras Indian museum, in the Tremé, the oldest Black neighborhood in the US, I came upon a group of construction workers sitting under an awning in the shade, in the afternoon heat, two Creole brothers in their fifties and one younger white man in his twenties who soon said his ancestors were from Cuba. I marveled at how brown white people can get in that radiating sun, skin saturated to all its potential, to leave us squinting at the continual racial ambiguity: and one of the reasons I love this city is I identify with those blurred boundaries, and people are more comfortable with it down here: it doesn't piss them off as much as most other places I've been, well not in the same way, anyway.

I told them I liked the house across the street, its cool, gray-blue, and I wanted to take a picture of it, and it turned out to belong to one of the two older brothers. Soon, the conversation came to Katrina, without any natural segue, in that telling way that you know a matter sits with great heaviness on someone's mind, your friend's obtuse connections to his ex-wife over dinner, the weight of the non-sequitur, most revealing thing in the world. Paul asked if I had seen Spike Lee's film about Katrina. I had, but the truth is, I don't remember it well because I think I watched it when I was exhausted. He said he'd been in it. He said, "We got two thousand people out. Then they stopped us at gun point. Sent me to Nebraska."

They turned people back at the highway with attack dogs. They left people to die for four days. We could have saved ourselves, but they stopped us. He was a thin man, his limbs floated out of his sleeves, his plaid shorts, furry with gold hair gleaming in the sun, all knees and elbows. He said he would never fly the American flag again. He pointed to where a small cloth skull and cross bones image hung off of his roof. "That's my flag now. I ain't no American." He said he was a veteran who'd once flown a flag. He'd been a soldier in Vietnam.

I wanted to ask if Obama changed anything. I wondered if that had provided any sense of relief to Black New Orleanians' view of this country. I had been wondering that since I arrived, but for some reason I found it a difficult question to ask, just as I found it difficult to explain that I was researching for a project about miscegenation, writing about Creoles of color, and how they got that way, the fucking and the love affairs, the astounding number of both common-law-marriage and concubines, and the undeniable generations of rape.

I am clearly not from Louisiana once I open my mouth though I have been told I look something like people down here. I'm an American, born here, citizenship from birth. I come from miscegenation. I am also from a country colonized twice, by Northern and Southern European cultures and I am writing something at the center of myself: the intersection of sex and power and color. I have my education, I am of the first world, because the women in my family married white. And here is a city built of such tales; they exist throughout the Americas but this is the one in the U.S., where some of the truth is told. And New Orleans may well be the seat of our culture. If this is the city where cool was born, this may well be the seat of our aesthetic.

Feeling vulnerable, I did not tell them what I was doing. I am afraid to hear it's not my place, that is always my fear, although no one in my whole trip had ever said anything like that. And I let my questions about Obama go unasked. Did these two brothers, born, I would guess, in the early 50s know anything of the African, the mixed-race women, the French, the Spanish men, who created their lineage?

I had been getting lonely and vulnerable of late, too long without people I know well, feeling not so much myself, not ready to converse or debate, so I let it all alone, too important to me. Ha! I recoil because I care too much.

The guy told me he was making his own film. He told me his full name, to remember it and keep an eye out for it. He pointed me to the Backstreet Cultural Museum, the Mardi Gras Indian Museum. I thought it was a family home, though I found out later it was an old funeral parlor which had been fixed up with grant money. The proprietor's brother was sitting in an awning, across the street, drinking bottled water. He walked with me to open up the place.

I had read a bit about the Mardi Gras Indian traditions long before I came down. They participate in long-standing rituals during the festival season, not in the parades, but as actions in Black neighborhoods around the city. The costumes are incredible, made of the brightest softest feathers of which you can conceive, with sequence and large shining beads, like tropical fish in some long unexplored ocean bottom crevice, some astounding miracle of evolution, of potentiality, imagination.

I had been enamored of colors my whole trip, but these costumes were a whole new level. They take a year to make, and members of gangs, or tribes, what they call the groups, get together pretty soon after Mardi Gras and start working on the next year's gear. They have various roles, Big Chief, Spy, Flag boy, and they move about the neighborhoods and when they meet another gang, there are elaborate rituals that are performed, complete with some language only they understand. It used to be that there was actual brawling, but nowadays, as I understand, the people involved work very hard to keep it a positive cultural inheritance. There are contests, arguments over who has the prettiest costumes and because the population was in diaspora, they are working hard extra hard to pass it on to the youngsters.

So the man, a man in his fifties, muscular from labor, bald, dark-skinned, missing some teeth, shows me about a dozen costumes exhibited around a long thin room. They're from 2002 until the present, missing 2005. He explained the various officers. And I stood there: True Orange. Emerald Greene. Pure Yellow. Rich Purple. The most perfect red, redder than any previous red I'd ever seen, red turned up like the shiniest costume jewelry, but soft, feathers with a belly, a headpiece of sequence and large plastic, light-reflecting beads. Grown, masculine, men loving the soft and fluffy, like girl children, in touch with the most basic emotions, emotions men are trained their whole lives to denigrate. There were what seemed like a dozen costumes, chiefs and sidemen from the new millennium.

To the left was another room with memorabilia, photographs of earlier Indians and the Zulu Kings, laminated explanations laid out in large, readable font, glass cases full of scepters and articles and the coconuts the Zulus toss out during the parade. I asked the man about the origins of the whole thing, and what he answered was what I had theorized, was what I had seen reflected in the desire to create the softest prettiest object that can be worn. "The Indians, some of them used to take in runaway slaves," he said.

The man left me alone for a moment, and I stood there in the center of the room, in the center of a dozen of the prettiest things I'd ever seen in my life. I knew I'd be back. I decided when the inevitable tragedy came: the loss of family, a relationship, some disappointment I could barely stand. At some midpoint of recovery, six months, a year later, I would come back to this room and get my optimism back, say: I'm ready to live again. Some people feel moved by mountains and rolling valleys, the Grand Canyon, the ocean, but for me it's this man-made imitation of glorious sunsets and ducklings, all pulled together here in warrior garb, some epic tale of love and hate, with love winning.

And I'm still, after all these years, half way through my life expectancy, not sure I believe in God, though I'm open to it now, as I wasn't ten years ago, because life is harder now and I need to feel there is something that connects me. It just feels better to believe, and I believe that if there is a God, he is diametrically opposed to large, gray, bureaucracy, as cesspool from rainbow.

The Germans, soon after the Holocaust admitted what had happened, they had no choice. And the Germans I've known in New York, we meet everyone in New York, World City, are in general embarrassed, or at least clearly renounce their grandparents' generation. I do not believe that a generation should feel ashamed for their forefathers' evils. Instead, it's the truth that is so important. A truth that says: this is obscenity. This is the converse of humanity. It is the truth that is necessary to really bring full citizenship to those, of us, who feel alienated because the denial is lingering insult. It happened here, as ugly as Nazis, much larger in scale and with reverberations that continue violently into Obama's America.

In this room, in this museum, in this family's home in the Tremé in New Orleans, I felt like I had arrived at some truth I'd needed all along and it felt like home to me, my American self, the meeting place of three peoples bursting against each other in the cyclone of history, two continents (or four) and two of those three peoples perhaps known but certainly denied: the unsung, the stubborn, the radiant. Ships at a distance. Capacity for wonder. Apocalypse and Holocaust. Holocaust. Apocalypse. And I will not leave you with an image of the dispossessed, wandering up the roadway, the undead groping up the roadway after the dead, the disease, the rotting innards, the search for nourishment. Nor will I leave you with an image of the genius instruments of torture, its iron rods and orderly systems. Nor the terror, the wild eyes of the bewildering unknown. I will leave you with the image of beloved warriors on horseback, cherishing their families, protecting their neighbors, riding into the Next World, fierce like deities, gentle as poets, soft as hatchlings, as magnificent as every last dusk.

The Glory of

Given the deeply troubled soul of Iron Mike, it made perfect sense. Once it did happen, it seemed the only thing that could have happened. I recognized the emotional logic behind the events. The outcome was both fantastically new and what I had, on some level, known all along.

I had become intrigued after the first fight, and my own predictions had flip-flopped moments before they entered the ring. I had believed for months that Tyson would take it because he *had* to win. He had much more at stake than Holyfield. If Tyson were to lose the rematch, this would mean that his years in prison had destroyed him, that there were forces stronger than his own will. This is an unnerving idea for anybody, but for one who realistically aspires to be the world's toughest man, the possibility is horrifying.

I changed my mind about what would happen as soon as I saw their faces. I was not certain Tyson was scared. I was not quite sure what that concentrated look contained, but there was no doubt in my mind that Holyfield was not. He sauntered in on his choice of funky gospel music, and he was rapturous. He was in the throes of ecstasy, the Glory Of. Yes, there was not a trace of doubt on that prince's face. It was all just too good to be true.

And for Tyson who had made a life of scaring the shit out of his opponents, this serenity of Holyfield's was a truth that must not be. After they leaned on each other like marathon dancers, in that intriguing, passionate moment of rest boxers take, even after Tyson swung his mouth around, still like a lover, and left a bloody sliver of a moon in Holyfield's ear, the defending champion only lost his cool for thirty seconds, and then returned to his peace. Yes, Tyson could not humiliate Holyfield and thus Tyson was humiliated. Until that moment I had not had a preference for the winner. I had had my predictions without rooting for anyone. But Holyfield was forever bestowed nobility after the bites, and I felt pity for Tyson. It felt like what must be, the Horrible Truth. What it represented intrigued me. Had Tyson lost his will? Had he willed his own failure? Had he engineered a reinstigation of terror, or was it the power of myth to begin with?

Six weeks ago, I began to sleep every other night. After three weeks, sleeping pills worked, and after four, unless I doubled the dosage, they did not. I have become afraid of addiction, so I have quit taking pills and accepted that this may go on for some time. The night after I sleep, I am so grateful that I experience some of the sweetest, highest highs I have known. This— gratitude, for me, is synonymous with happiness.

The night I do not sleep, or the night I wake up thirty-five minutes into my nightmares— (rabid dogs, teeth pulled, rodents, gray, always gray, raw sewage, the brute brute heart of the night) I experience a despair which I cannot convey to the uninitiated. Let us just say, I better understand Poe, that no grief, no mourning, ever felt like this.

This all makes no sense. The therapist wants to discuss my family. Yes, I had a difficult childhood. Perhaps there was less love and more anger than there should have been. And yet, I have known much worse beginnings for much happier people.

I try to fathom this force which rage rage rages in my veins. I don't even try to sleep anymore when it has hit me, for to lie down while my adrenaline refuses to stop, it's wrenching. You will think I'm insane. I used to laugh at insanity.

Sleep: it is a pellet which bursts open inside the brain where the neck curves into the fullest part of the skull. It is a circular shape, more flat than spherical, like an M&M, but smaller and more powerful. That drug-released, melatonin, I think, is its technical name. It's related to orgasm; this I know. It's delicious. It's all I ask.

They say be careful what you wish for because you might get it. I sold my work, finally, for what I consider a significant amount of money. Not enough to last forever, but enough to quit my jobs for the summer and stare out the window, thinking. It was this monster, some kind of seizure. And I would turn to Tommy, my husband, my first and only love, I would turn to him, with the helplessness of a child, my arms outstretched. It's coming to get me, I would say. At first, he would wrap his arms around me, and I could see love and fear in his face.

It turns up the speed on my blood, while the earth stands still and the city sprints about at its usual pace. I shake, and there are less stresses than ever before. My fingers worm about excitedly. I feel continually as if I've just woken to a sound in the dark.

This is everything I've ever hated. If you are like me, if you believe what I have believed for most of my life, you will be disgusted. What I need is some hard work to subdue an overactive imagination. This is the disease of the bourgeois— the hyperactive cousin to ennui, the vapors, too much time on one's hands. I called it, when I was a young and struggling artist, the Trust Fund Casualty. Too much money for Prozac and the endless conviction that The Answer is out there, the wish to relinquish to something greater than one's own Will, Not now in the bible but in Freud or a feminist successor. I knew those girls in school. They screamed *help* and somebody *helped* them. Their costly therapies and relaxation techniques. Their weakness disgusted me. I was jealous and righteous. I knew how to survive, keep moving. It is really not so bad.

Yes, for me, happiness is synonymous with gratitude, and life's greatest gift is the capacity to love.

My heart, and God knows how this happened, was shut until I was thirty. I'm telling you, I don't know how to explain it. I lived in anger, and if I laughed, it was derisive, for all my young life. If I had friends, they were partners in derision. How my heart opened is a miracle, and for four solid years, I looked at the sky in wonder. Tommy taught me how to love.

Looking at the circumstances of his life, there is no rhyme or reason why he has always known how to greet the world with unabashed affection. This quality was there from the start. There is proof. His family tells stories. I have seen photographs of his exuberant face as a child.

There were five of them, five boys and Tommy was the third. He was by no means the smartest nor most handsome, and today, is nowhere near the most successful, but by the time he was three, his mother tells me, he had this way of meeting every person's eyes with joy and intimacy. He met every person's eyes as if they were his special friend.

There are his brothers, the spoiled lot of them, the sadistic and devilishly handsome group of them. Technically speaking, Tommy is the least attractive. His chin is weaker, his body every-so-slightly misshapen, shoulders narrower than a man should hope for himself. But it's that gaze, that first meeting of the eyes. He greets you with the bravery of a child. He never fears for the response.

Imagine them in a receiving line, the second eldest has been married, five of them in a row. First, the youngest, who still has the arrogance of potential, he smiles with his broad white teeth, he moves athletically, clasps the elbow as he grips the hand, but there is something false in this. And he wants you to know, this callous rockstar, wants you to know that he's faking it. Hello, how are you, he says, nodding like a kitchen ornament. The second, he is more like me, eyes averted. Doesn't want to know, doesn't care to know, has friends of his own and they are not here. He gets through this by contemplating his friends' fierce loyalty, his partners in derision. He'll tell his friends how awful we all were, passing through the receiving line. Our horrible taste and irrelevant small talk. The eldest is fourth. Today he is jealous. He has never cared to be married, never thought of it, but today, he notices that the younger did so first. Now, he wants a beautiful woman, a beautiful, beautiful, woman. He keeps looking at the clock and scouring the crowd for Someone Else.

The groom has a feeling of dread he expects to pass. He wants to drink. But Tommy, we passed Tommy in the middle. Tommy, with his running, tumbling smile. Many of us had an impulse to turn around and see who that look of recognition was actually for. Many a woman felt she was special to him.

There was a time when I was so very unafraid that I simply gave over to watching my mind wander. I wasn't afraid of any nook or cranny of my memory. If I awoke in the middle of the night, I considered it luck that I had the opportunity to see what my thoughts would land upon. It was the most unpredictable adventure. I could think of my own family, and I had understanding. I wasn't embarrassed by my own behavior. Anything from the-days-before-Tommy was adolescent, was to be smiled upon, was all part of the story of me and then us.

I had empathy. I could *see* the moods of others. I developed this technique: when I experienced the negative emotion, and then the negative behavior, of people around me, I would scour my brain until I'd recalled something similar in myself. Usually, it would work. It might take days of thinking, but it would work. Then I could forgive the person, and then, I could forgive myself.

My friends, our friends: Paul, who loved to argue— who, even if asked directly; Paul, see if you can go half an hour tonight, see if you can refrain from contradicting whatever I say. Paul, who couldn't help himself, and so he'd buy you dinner or help you paint to compensate. Randy, whose skill was listening, who remembered the names from all your stories and asked about them later. Mona the martyr, who would sooner fetch your muffin for you. Our kind and deeply idiosyncratic friends. And the girls in the coffee shop, and the eyes I would meet on the subway— smiling with another thirty something woman over the teen globbing on makeup next to me. All day long, in this subtle way, I befriended perfect strangers. A life of slight grins and laughter.

My one sorrow was that a life such as this had been there all along and I had failed to notice it. And yet I had noticed it. It was so simple and insurmountable at once. And then it was insurmountable again.

Barbara was having a party for the fight and invited us. I like boxing, but I don't like Barbara. My various techniques of connection haven't worked for her. Let's not go, sweetheart, I said. Please, let's not go. Tommy, whose very gestures make me think of biting into the sweet, dense meat of fresh fruit. Tommy has developed a tic of intolerance.

And why, he answered. A statement. Why, sigh, not.

All I want now, is to hang on to life. I feel, what it is, at the heart of this monster, is that my relationship to human life is more precarious than it ever was, and I had been, those years ago, so very alone. Even Tommy, giver of all gifts, I can *feel* his resistance to my swallowing need. Mona doesn't want to see me. There is nothing more repulsive than overwhelming need.

Barbara, there's this quality to her, I can't put my finger on it. It's those phone messages— her voice is so controlled, and saccharine. Evil, her voice is evil, and Tommy sighs.

No, really, there is that quality. She is always about to snicker. She would forget what I had just said, constantly, and then gaze directly on me, about to snicker. It's sadistic. That's the quality, sadism.

And she doesn't love her husband. That is clear. She never looks him in the face. Her eyes land everywhere but on his face and when he speaks, you can see her cringe, you can see that she detests him enough that she doesn't care if she humiliates him. She takes apart his arguments with her rolling eyes. She makes him look like a fool. And I hate not so much for that cruelty, but for the cowardliness of staying on with a man she doesn't love.

I have always liked boxing. I don't know very much about it, or understand it very well, but the few fights that I have watched have struck me. Boxers look to me so fantastically exalted and alone. For this reason, though they must feel themselves, with good reason, the strongest most daring athletes of all, they are also, in their aloneness, the most vulnerable. We can read their faces and guess at their state of mind like we cannot other athletes, who move too quickly and are lost in crowds. And now a days, we hear every last thing the fighter's trainer says to egg him on: *Your son will know you lost this fight. Do you want your son to know you are a loser?* The urgency. I respond to this.

And so, we go to the party. Barbara answers the door and gazes at us with her maniacal, salivary smile. Her hair is coifed and she inhales so that her breasts rise. Tommy gives her his inspirational greeting and I do the best I can.

There is no position I can take in the living room that is comfortable. People who hover about, they know the cues of conversation, when to leave a cluster, when to join one, cues I no longer understand. And so I slide myself onto the crowded couch behind a woman I once knew quite well. I sit behind her back. She is busy talking to someone else, and so it is easy to sit and not be responsible for socializing. It is easy for me to simply stare into space. My brain works that way these days. Tommy brings me some black olives on napkins and tells me how exquisite they are, and goes back to talk to others.

This is not, of course, just Tyson's fight, but the preliminary fights are generally ignored. A few more interested fans try to shush the guests to no avail until Chavez. The commentators generally agree that he is past his prime, though he is thirty-five, one year older than Holyfield, the reigning champion, one year older than a man, who has come of age at thirty-four. There is a general ruckus because he's fighting a tall, skinny never-been who puts up aluminum siding part time in Wisconsin. People are drunk now, and fancy themselves wits. *Pummel that aluminum siding dude. Look at that elongated motherfucker. I could take him out. I'm gonna call that guy when this is over I need some work done.* And Chavez does pummel the aluminum siding guy, and this feels very unjust. Someone explains to me how they come up with these last-minute victims who know they're going to lose, how they save a guy like Chavez for a specific fight. They probably called the aluminum siding guy two weeks ago. No, I think, but don't articulate, no, he doesn't know he's going to lose. He doesn't think that. This is it. This is his Miracle.

Tommy comes out of the kitchen with a glass of white wine in each hand, we both drink white wine. He always does the right thing, spends a party fetching me things for everyone to see. Barbara comes out of the kitchen behind him, and something absurd happens. She mirrors his movements. I don't know how it happens because she doesn't seem to be looking at him, but as his head sweeps slowly to the left, hers does, and when he pauses and scans the couch for me, so does she. Both of her arms are bent to the same angle as his, although one of her hands is empty, and has no reason to be bent. It is like some childish game of mockery. Like a bad actor, who moves as she moves without really doing what she's doing.

Tommy delivers my wine. There is no seat for him near me, the leaning space on the floor against the couch is all taken. He stands in the kitchen doorway. And so. And another one who fancies himself a wit, he says: *Christians and Muslims, what is this, Bosnia?* and everybody laughs. And then, the short fight, and Tyson bites Holyfield's earlobe off, and I, even my disengaged self, I have an amazing feeling of disbelief, I have that feeling I get, that one gets in the age of VCRs, the instant urge to rewind, but they will do it for us enough, soon to come, them, the commanders of information.

There was a time, when I figured the only way to make a person love us is to know they will. It's amazing. We cannot *believe*, that is not good enough, we have to *know*. We can't walk out into the world of the searching hoping to make them truly love us. This is repulsive. One has to know and fear they will. One has to feel eyes upon us and know what it means. And I never knew that in my young life, and so I never had love.

Sometimes, sometimes in my thinking, I believe my magic life was conceived not with Tommy, but the moment before Tommy, somehow, in that evening, the fateful place spot space where his eyes came upon me, somehow in the instant before, I knew I was lovable and then saw that Tommy was the one to do it. Sometimes, I believe that that inconceivable joy, those jolts of cool adrenaline from inexplicable sources came the instant before him. And the young woman next to me is blabbering, imitating Tyson's effeminate lisp, and I look over at Tommy, and he is saying to someone what everyone is saying, my god can you believe this, my god, look at that asshole, and I know that Tommy does not love me anymore.

The Other Realm

She was not my kind of woman. That much was clear. This is the irony of the situation. I mean, my friends have been by-and-large, brunettes, though that is not the defining characteristic. Women with hips and bite to their manner of speaking. Immigrants of this century and not the last, and nearly always but a generation away from the motherland. Guyana, the Philippines, Mexico, Iran, Italy, Israel— yes, I have kept company with many a Jewess. I grew up with a Native American girl who was adopted by a white family. I am very fond of a rebel daughter of Korean doctors. I'm sometimes one of the yellower faces at Black women's parties. And even the exceptions have been for other reasons, unique in our circles. I palled around for several years with Maja, the Finnish lesbian, and then there was Heidi, the 6'2 redhead.

No matter how kind a woman you are, you are never a good girl if you're cynical. You're cynical if you feel you've been betrayed.

We err on the side of passion. We regret what we have done and not what we have not. Though there is a limit to this. I have learned how to spot the selfishly destructive and the bullies.

Paula. She was not the girl I would have sat next to in school. She was prim and slender and pale. I always felt a bit obscene next to her.

If she was Jane Eyre then I was the madwoman, the id to her superego. She was my boss. I stuffed envelopes. She was in charge of publicity. This was public television, and so there was a feeling of moral imperative behind the decisions made in that place. She was good. She was a good, good girl.

Though I was very depressed that summer, I managed to make friends. I sat in the back, in the stock room, doing the publicity mailings. Perhaps because she was much younger than me and I was therefore not as nervous as I was apt to be at the time, I befriended Mitrah, who was from the Midwest like myself, and whose family had fled Iran. She was the Outreach Intern, and we started with "The Tsarina of Outreach" and went on to "The Tsarina of Soul" and stopped when Paula tiptoed back and asked, politely, for she always spoke politely, if we would mind keeping it down and perhaps we could move along with our tasks.

I disliked her intensely and I wanted desperately for her to like me. She seemed to like everybody in the office but me. In most cases, this made sense. Except for the producers, they were quiet and studious women. They sat in their cubicles raising funds or organizing meetings and even when they argued, it was barely distinguishable from conversation and their voices were warm, high, feminine murmurs. Yes, Paula walked through with her blondish brown hair pinned up, saying hello, meaning it sincerely and even when she greeted Mitrah, who was mine, who was *like me*, there was a warmth to her smile.

When she smiled toward me, there was a difference. It was barely perceptible. Her mouth took the same shape, formed the same words, but a single element, we might name it affection, disappeared. How I was able to sense this, I cannot prove to you. A recoil occurred, so tiny and slight that it is indescribable.

I brought it up with Mitrah once. "Paula doesn't like me," I said. "Don't be silly," responded my friend with her dismissive hand.

I began trying too hard. I spoke to her awkwardly. My voice went up a bit. I acted dumb so that she could be the expert. *Oh, really?* I made unnatural small talk. I stood hovering, thinking of things to say. I pretended to be interested in things I wasn't and I always stood an extra beat after she answered my inquiries. I stood there a moment expecting more after she explained her weekend, as if in that next moment would come proof of her love, as if the next would undo this. I walked by her office and exchanged smiles. It was the same smile every time, with that indescribable falsity, that pea in the mattress. I told myself to stop. I told myself to retreat. The only thing that ever works is to disappear, or show that we are offended, allow for guilt, and somehow, these commonsensical ideas, they were impossible. I was fixated.

It became worse and worse. I couldn't help myself. Would you like some of my sun-dried tomato spread? Would you like to join Mitrah and me for a drink on Friday? The single most humiliating episode "Paula, my god, is that a *hickey*?" And it was a bit strange that I could see the thing at all, I was at the copy machine. She was a few good paces away, but her collar opened with a stretching motion, and I saw it, the purple splotch. It was large. It seeped over her neck, onto her shoulder. I must have seen it before. "Do you have a new boyfriend you're not telling us about?" I mean, the thing was the size of my fist.

"Oh," she said distractedly, walking past with an unlabeled file, "No, that's an old childhood...."

When I am happy, sleep and its surrounding moments are a delicious delicious gift. Sleep, my subtle adventure, more exciting and unexpected than what the natural world offers. I could wake in the middle of the night, and not have it bother me. I could lie there, and watch where my thoughts went and discover why my mother was angry that day seventeen years before. I could suddenly imagine the city of Prague or an affair with a movie star. I arrive vividly in conversation from the morning or a party from my college years. And dreams— the only thing better than dreams is love and the third best thing is recalling in the morning and noticing intricacies.

And of course, when I am unhappy, all of this is lost. Lying down in the evening is a dreadful thing because all there is the bold and looming face of the wound. The sleep itself is okay, is less bad than the rest, but to wake, to leave this half-peace, is a return to the ache, and dreams, well they are full of anxiety.

I lost my taste for sleep that summer night when Ernesto did not arrive home until late. I tried not to wait up for him. I have never wanted to be that kind of woman, but I could not concentrate on TV or a book and in no way shape or fashion did my mind wander when I tried to end the day. I sat on the edge of the bed smoking and imagining rivals. When it came to Ernesto, I was not jealous of the most beautiful girls, but simply the most petite and refined. He was smaller than me. Though he liked loudness and cynical stories, there was something in his very bone structure which made me wonder if he wouldn't prefer someone light and precise and graceful. His wrists were half the size of mine, and his legs. It was no issue when we made love, I loved him relentlessly, but when we danced in public, I would become suddenly aware of the difference.

The first evening he came home late, which has to happen, there will be a first time after the initial intensity, an evening in which one of the lovers loves their friends and their freedom as well— I sat on the edge of the bed smoking and waiting for his key in the lock. I had it set up so I could snub out the thing and shove the ashtray under the bed quickly enough. I counted on him being too drunk to notice the smell of a recent cigarette. And I was right. I listened to the key and his heavier disoriented steps. He drank a glass of water and then used the bathroom. I pulled the sheet up in time and lay still. He came to me, fitted himself around me and fell into unconsciousness. I lay there all night wondering if this were the turning point.

In the morning I had a talk with myself. You must not do this, I said. This will be the Ruin of Everything.

To be a failed artist is to hurt a little bit every day. There are the weeks or months of more profound blows, and then there is that dull and constant ache. Sometimes you make note of it, and sometimes you don't but it is always there.

When I turned twenty-eight, I changed my mind. Part of it was that I was embarrassed by my shit jobs. I started to want to know how old everyone was. Then I could forgive myself somewhat every time there were a handful of fellow-employees my own age. Or I would tell myself stories of how old so-and-so was when he made it.

I grew tired of hiding. I hid from people who had started out with me and surpassed. I hid from people who doubted me and when I was at my worst, I hid from anyone who might ask for a progress report including my own family.

But the deciding factor was that I had never been in love. Not really, a bit here or there, something on the long-term back in school, but I wanted to know what it felt like, that other realm. And I knew that as long as I was a failure I would be incapable. I was too bitter and defensive to *glow* into anyone.

And so I quit. I threw up my hands. Okay, *you were right*, and I went from being an artist to an employee and after I bottomed out for a bit, then I was relieved. On some level I knew this would happen all along and then I met Ernesto.

The next evening, after he came home late, I had promised myself not to be ridiculous, and I knew I would sleep easily that night because I was exhausted. I would even go to bed hours before him which would show my independence.

But then when Nesto came home, he was nervous. When he was nervous, he could not make conversation. I remember feeling reluctant on our first few dates, because he seemed unable to think of things to say. Unless I initiated with questions, all he could do was repeat some part of what I had said. And that night, he came home straight from work and we cooked and I talked.

"It's this never ending smile, I swear."

"Never ending."

"Yeah, when you first meet her, you think it's demonic, I swear. But then. You get to know her…."

"Demonic."

And then later he made love to me like he was sorry. I lay awake.

On the third night, I would certainly sleep. How could I not? I was half crazed. I stuffed envelopes, thinking in circles. I called myself every name in the book, and envied the fact that Ernesto had work which took concentration. I made plans to better myself. And I did it. I went to sleep before him and I moved instantly into intense and vivid dreams. I woke when he pressed himself gently against me, and I fell asleep again.

I remember the dream. I was lying on the back of a flat bed truck, hiding, driving over infinite highways. We were traveling between nations. I was with a man. He was a redhead but he was swarthy. He was a big, muscular man. I was both man and woman at the same time. I was this man's companion as a woman. He protected me from the rest, from all the other men who wanted to rape me as a man. I loved him out of gratitude and feared him.

I was dreaming this. I was in the heart of it, somehow realizing its depth, both audience and participant and it was, I was somehow aware, the sleep to save my sanity and I awoke with a yank up up up to the surface.

My adrenaline was raging. I felt a burning sensation between my fingers, and I watched as a splotch, a huge insect bite swelled up on the loose skin joining pointer finger and thumb. The bite itself was not so painful but it was as if a poison had entered my blood stream, its only mission to wake me, warn me, I suppose. It seemed an impossible cruelty. I looked around the room for the culprit and saw a tiny, fragile bit of gray hovering before the shades. I drew myself out of bed as carefully as I could, leaving Nesto in his peace and I, how silly it was, held my open hands toward the thing as if I could kill it in a clap. I chased it until I lost it.

There were other bites. I would feel the burn first. On the inside of my ankle, and then I would watch the welt form. My elbow, behind my ear. I had about seven of them. I shook my limbs out trying to cool myself. I inspected Ernesto. He had one on his jaw but he did not stir.

A thin, light and even initiation of panic spread under my skin. Just the very seed, but flat and even. I could do nothing but sit on a chair in the kitchen. I tilted the chair back until it leaned against the wall. That felt right. I could do nothing but sit there and smoke and hope that whatever it was in my bloodstream quickly left. I heard people come into the building, shuffle about in their apartments getting ready for bed. The girl next door must have been a waitress, for at times, I heard her, as I did that night, come home late and she always took a shower. I counted the people I truly trusted in the world. People I could imagine pacing in the hallway if I were in the hospital. There were four, and three of them lived in distant cities.

I heard everything that night. The garbage truck taking our three cans downstairs. The acceleration of cars after the nearby stoplight. Cable wires knocking against the side of the building. And strangely enough, I heard the whistle of trains all night and I had no idea where the tracks were. I didn't think we were anywhere near any tracks at all.

There was something slightly sour in my mucous and I was sure that I would taste the difference as the bites faded, and I was right. It was very nearly dawn, it must have been five then, and a very consoling exhaustion swept over me. I crawled back into bed, thinking I would call in sick. But it woke me again, that perverse little insect, that instant of my suffering. It got me again. All it took was one bite this time, on the smooth underneath of my forearm. I resigned myself to this strange state between a hyper sensitivity and delirium. I mean that poison somehow, it turned up the volume on everything, the lights brightening as well, and at the same time, I felt that if I tried to speak, I would make no sense. Incoming was shrewd. Outgoing was thick and muddled. I sat on the tilted back chair. I watched and waited. I said. This will pass. I said. Hold yourself together.

And yes, on the way to work, for I had to work, what else would I do, would I sleep all day and be up all night again? On the way to work, how dirty everything seemed. How much more prominent the cracked tiles in our building, the brown-orange muck that gathered. The smell of coffee and eggs from the diners and bodegas, also the smell of urine. And the sun— as if this were long, flat land, the desert, and the sun rising in just the direction I needed to walk. Yes, coming up between the buildings, it rose as if it were full, interrogating. I had to shield my eyes against it.

And I know I puzzled Mitrah. I buried my head in the stock room as if my work took concentration. For I felt tender. I felt as tender as a bruise. Swollen and ready to burst. I could be touched yes, but the wrong touch and I would burst and that would be very embarrassing. Yes, Mitrah, she came in and hovered there behind me, saying she'd been out the night before, wanting to tell me a story. She'd met someone perhaps, or something amusing had happened, something she felt I would understand. But I did not want to talk, I couldn't. I said hello. I gave enough to be polite but I kept my back to her. I counted things as a trick to pass time. I would fold one hundred pamphlets, stuff one hundred envelopes and then close the hundred envelopes with a sponge. The next round I would do fifty.

And at moments I lifted my head, yes, I felt nearly liquid. And I inhaled and held the air in my lungs until I felt just a bit larger. That was a bit soothing. Mitrah asked me what was wrong, and I let her know, with a motion, that it was better to leave me alone.

I could not eat my lunch as the chicken tasted of chemicals and when I came back, I went straight back to Paula's office. I walked in carefully. As quietly as I could so no one would look up and speak to me. I had to brace myself and say, that yes, I would probably appear very nervous. I had to accept the fact that my voice would do strange things and I might cry. I told myself that this was okay.

I knocked. Come in, she said, cheerily. She looked up and then, seeing my face, she took on an expression of concern. It bothered me. It was condescending, as if I were that weak, and she my mother. This frail and boyish woman. But I couldn't stop. I sat down in that wheeled chair and pushed myself up to her with my toes. I had trouble speaking and I did not look her in the face.

"Paula,"

"Yes," she touched me comfortingly. I cringed.

"Why don't you like me?"

I knew I had mumbled and would have to repeat myself. I inhaled and held. I rephrased. I said, "Why do you dislike me?"

Her eyebrows pinched together. She rubbed my knee.

"I don't dislike you," she said, as if she were surprised, that tone. I cringed again. And you know, we don't communicate through words, not at all, we communicate through a million subtle actions of the body and what she really said, for *I don't dislike you* was what a polite woman must say, what she really said, with that slight tone of intolerance, that tiny sigh of frustration, what she really said was *because you so foolishly let me.*

Godspeed

The James Baldwin short story, "Sonny's Blues" is about two brothers who grew up in Harlem during the Second World War. One, the eldest, is a bit righteous, an upstanding-citizen type, a teacher and a family man. The other is a jazz musician and a heroin addict. The parents died while they were young, and the eldest tried to be a father to the youngest, but could never care for him in the way that he wanted. The algebra instructor, he is only slightly more disgusted with the pianist than he is with himself, and disapproves sadly, mistrustfully, for most of the work.

But then, at the very end, the older brother, who is the narrator, goes to see the younger, whose name is Sonny, perform. The narrator, who remains nameless, enters this higher realm, this golden room, in which Sonny's "veins bore royal blood." The music is sublime and the narrator somehow makes peace, at least for that moment, with the trials they've suffered.

But what I find most moving about the work, is Sonny's relationship with another musician, the bassist, name of Creole. Creole: aged, but not ancient, borne of the Americas, first bastard child of the Empire, and here, now, in the golden room— the Father Sonny's brother could never be. He is the eldest of the musicians and the leader, and when Sonny plays the piano, in a way the narrator never could, he looks on, with a pure unadulterated love and wishes him "godspeed."

Yes, and when I read that story I was breaking up with a man for whom I felt very much, but who was not quite right for me. I was walking about making mental lists of the things I felt were absolutely necessary. An openness, intelligence, an emotional honesty, a sense of humor, and the wish for godspeed.

And so, of course, after Tommy and I were well on our way, when we huddled together and had those few whispering inches between us, when we lived and breathed in those few infinite inches, I told him about that story and that I had set out to find a man who sincerely wished success for me. Yes, he said. And I really, truly felt, that if Tommy could hold me in his cupped hands and toss me into the sky, if he could do that and know it would make me happy, he would.

It has always been one of my worst fears that no man could take a woman more successful than he. This may strike you as silly, or ironic. Silly, because I suppose most young artists worry, first of all, about whether they will be successful in the first place, never mind that other, later shit, cross that bridge when we get to it. But I worried from the start. When I was younger I was very naive about the whole thing. I thought they who failed secretly willed it upon themselves. And silly because most any sociological observation will break down under scrutiny. It is like saying women only want men at least so many inches taller than themselves.

The reason for irony will soon unfold.

We don't always know when we are pushing another person's buttons. I have a dear friend who gets the creeps, more than the rest of us, when the conversation turns to insanity. Her mother was mentally ill and she spent two years, the last of high school and the first year after, terrified that *it* was beginning with her. We can be among others, she and I, we could be sitting at a round table over beers with people we know well but not as well as each other, and the conversation can veer off into someone or other's psychotic episode and it is as if I can feel her temperature go up, her vertigo begin and I will be the only other one at the table who senses it.

And once, I had no idea, Tommy and I had been to see a band and I had known the ex-girlfriend of one of the musicians and I mentioned to him that the sax player was reputedly a junky. Hours later, we walked home in the rain and he threw his arm around me and made a request. He said: do me a favor and don't tell me about people's drug addictions. It scares me. I had thought his quiet that evening had been peaceful. But after he said that, I looked back, and the discomfort made sense.

And me. To this day, I feel panicked when I hear stories of men being unable to take a woman excelling. A sit com character breaks up with his girlfriend because she beats him at chess and I am stewing for hours afterward. I remember, still, years later, the interview I read with a starlet who said that making more money than your man is like a cancer. I hate that woman and her boyfriend.

And I know that everything we dislike is something which hurts us.

Tommy took off. One minute we were struggling, not too badly, I mean, working hard, dreaming of *when,* a bit tired but we had what we needed, and then suddenly, people knew who he was. I mean, in the circles we traveled in, anyway, and somewhat outside. He became important. Everything changed.

The desire for a successful man is astronomical. They didn't care if I was standing right there. They took his hand and squeezed it meaningfully. They held his eye contact a little too long— people I thought were my friends. I held on to his elbow and felt like dead weight. This too shall pass, I said. I felt myself diminishing, whittling down. I knew I was thinking of him all day long and he was not thinking of me. My main goal became to hide my desperation.

The worst of it was that he became so busy. He was off in the world receiving praise, doing his thing, making money and I was at home staring at the walls. And when he was with me, he was only thinking of going back out there where they showered him with admiration. My venues became meaningless. I grew ashamed of my B-class successes. What the hell were they worth?

How can I explain to you how he once loved me?

The ruin of everything was initiated quite suddenly after I thought the worst of it was over. He was away and I had had a very stern talk with myself. This is a storm, I said. Weather the storm. I forced myself to go through certain motions, tried to enjoy things unrelated to him. I didn't. But I was proud of myself for trying. I called old friends. I thought of planning a trip with my sister.

I was very busy for a few days. I made sure every minute was filled, so that I could sleep like a rock at night, so that I wouldn't lay there thinking, so that I might be out when he called from his business trip. I had new regimen. I had a schedule to keep. I went to the gym, to work. I made the attempt to dive into my own artistry. I met friends later. I had a drink or two. It was a simple start. It is what we do when we resolve to make things better, but then I fell sick.

It was a feverish feeling. I didn't truly have a fever, but I felt weak. I went a bit dizzy when I stood. My stairs exhausted me. I called in sick and then lay on the bed, on our bed, using the remote until I was disgusted with myself. I could feel it creeping on, emotions too big, and in my slight heat, the haze, I felt desire.

I went out, sweating and feeling a bit cold, to get soup or groceries. I don't remember what. It was already dark. On the way back, I passed the home for pregnant teens, which was across the street and a bit up the block. We could see that building from our bathroom window, and sometimes I watched the way they leaned in groups out the fourth floor windows, as if it were a girls' school, as if they were Rapunzel. Sometimes a figure would waddle into the shadows elsewhere on the block, between buildings, around the corner, and smoke.

Now there was a theater for all the possible permutations of lovers' suffering. On many occasions, I had been mesmerized by the boyfriends coming to visit. They weren't allowed upstairs and then they would have those scenes out front— stand twelve paces apart, one or both unable to lift their heads. They might yell and curse and walk away and walk back and walk away and walk back. There's the one where she's angry at him, fuck you, where have you been? Her jaw is set and he holds her chin in his hands and says look at me, baby, look. They enjoy this tenderness. Sometimes they get sent away. Simple as that, she walks out front, folds her arm over her now womanly chest. She is without her jacket in the cold, not planning to stay, and says something and goes back in. He stands there stupefied. Sometimes they throw their arms around each other with intense love. Sometimes she cries. He never does. Sometimes they just take hands and start strolling, as if our block were the place for a stroll.

And I walked past there with my chills and heat and my slowness and there was somebody getting arrested outside the home for pregnant girls. He looked very fashionable, like a model, a Black kid, about nineteen, I would guess, tall and elegant and something in his manner less huge and macho than the other visiting young men. Something quiet in him. He had a shaved head and he was wearing jeans which fit, while the style was to wear them very over-sized. He had on a white t-shirt and a brown bomber jacket. He dressed like somebody older than himself.

He was huddled against the wall, crouched with his back to the cops. There were almost a dozen of them, two in uniform, and many in plain clothes, but very obvious. It was a Puerto Rican neighborhood and why else would all those big white men with long hair and fringe jackets be standing on the street? They stood there talking and laughing, their breath visible in the cold, their hands in their pockets. There was one Black woman with her hair pulled sloppily back on her head. She was petite and dressed like a homeless person but looked far too healthy for that role. That's the problem with undercover cops and actors. It's difficult for anyone to get as dirty, as ugly, as they need to be. It is hard for us to conceive of degradation unless we are truly experiencing it. We resist. We don't understand.

Anyway, the young man, I felt he was a quiet watcher like myself, because he didn't dress like the other young men. He looked like an outsider, and because I had never seen anyone be arrested in the way he was being arrested. He was huddled against the wall, crouched on his heels with his hands over his head, his back to them— and at first I thought it was out of fear that they'd hit him, but then I realized the scene— the police, they were far too calm for that to be an element. They were speaking to him coaxingly, from a distance. I could not hear what they said.

Then I realized what his expression was. Utter despair. The will to disappear. He made himself small with the logic of a child who thinks he will no longer exist if he closes his eyes.

Obviously the whole thing had been planned well in advance, so many of them around, waiting. Obviously, he loved her very much.

And I went home. And I sat on the edge of my bed and I missed Tommy and my skin felt hot. I felt like any normal sensation would be heightened and I was lonely and I wanted to be touched. I was furious with Tommy because he no longer wanted me in the way he once did. I felt for the young man, the quiet and watchful, who must have known this was coming all along. Who, on one level had resigned himself to whatever risk there was and yet found the fact that he was being arrested inconceivable. Who loved like he loved.

And then, mutely, quickly, I found my empathy to be an escape. I had, for those moments of watching, forgotten my own problems. It was possible to feel something somewhere else, an emotion outside of Tommy. And that sensation of falling, the closing the eyes and jumping the young man must have done, that stranger. That meant something to me.

I had this strange, flowing sensation of magnanimity. It occurred to me that if I turned elsewhere in the world, that I would unburden Tommy. It was as if a force beyond my control were operating, and I got dressed and went out to a club.

We purport that infidelity is an act committed in spite of the betrothed when it is, so often, so very usually, an act committed upon the betrothed. I don't need you I don't need you look look look I don't need you. Even if I imagined myself the only audience to my affair, its purpose was my own conception of independence. He was a ridiculous man.

I had been carried to the club, I had flowed over there on my sense of humanity but as soon as I arrived, I retracted. I became burningly self-conscious. I had come alone. I was sure everyone around me understood my intent and I was ashamed. I sat down on a stool at the endless, winding bar, and I refused to look at anyone. I set my jaw. Someone knew me. Someone said, hey, aren't you a friend of so and so? And I nodded defensively without really making note of my mysterious acquaintance. I refused to meet his eyes and I left him embarrassed at the silence. I had a few drinks before I allowed myself to look up and realize that nobody was watching me at all.

There are young men whose way of loving is wrought with anger. There are women too, but we are more familiar with the men. Eventually, through trial and error, I learned to spot and avoid these types, and the older I became the sillier they appeared to me. Their *huge* carriage. They approach women with this in mind *you're a sucker if you buy this shit who are you to believe me?* They work off the assumption that their terms of endearment are bullshit so that it is no insult if they are rejected. They work in sheer numbers and prey on the weak. But that was an evening in which a man like that would be of use to me. He would be very aggressive, once given the go ahead, strong assurance, and that would alleviate a bit of responsibility for myself. Also— he would thrive on the fact that we were cuckolding Tommy and I would feel no guilt for him, for I would very much dislike him.

And the one I sought, the one I saw there and had my eye on; he looked a bit like Tommy, in a vague way, like cousins or citizens of the same stalwart region, something similar in bone structure, proportion of head to torso. Their coloring within a certain range. I will say Tommy was much more handsome, but you don't have to believe me.

There was something a bit sickly about NotTommy. He was paler than he should have been, washed out, thirsty for sun. He had bags under his eyes, though he was significantly younger than myself. He looked like he took a lot of time with his grooming— the gel in his hair, his soft, ironed shirt. And his very posture spoke volumes. He held his head rolled back so that his neck was thickened. I looked at him until he caught me and then I looked away. I was raging with nerves. When he approached me, that expression on his face, it was more frozen laughter than a smile. And we spoke. And he bought me a drink. And we went elsewhere for more. As if this man were *somebody* to me, as if he were *a friend*, I told him my secrets. It was absurd, but you know, when you're down in there you have no judgment. You bring worse and worse on yourself. I said, "Dear Mr. Nameless NotTommy. I am heartbroken." No, really, I said, "My boyfriend will leave me. He doesn't love me anymore." I said it and my eyes watered and he faced me with that frozen laughter. He touched my hair and bought me a drink. He said, can I kiss your cheek? And he kissed my lips. And then we were mauling each other in the corner and I made myself do it and he nibbled my earlobe and whispered, "I'm gonna fuck you like a bitch."

Arrhythmia

Upstairs, there was a girl who cleaned compulsively all day and at all hours of the night. She didn't seem to have a job or a boyfriend. It was a slightly more than subtle arrhythmic knocking. It wasn't loud. It was just endless and arrhythmic. I could do nothing to get her to stop. Talking reasonably did nothing. Anger and pounding did nothing. We exchanged well-articulated notes. I tried to be empathetic. I told her that in my first apartment, my downstairs neighbors had asked me not to walk so loud. This is true. It is also true that I changed my way of walking to accommodate them. I'm that kind of person. She wrote back, in extremely neat hand, with perfect roundness where necessary, that in her first apartment in New York, her upstairs neighbors were really loud but that she knew she had no right to tell them how to live. She was a short, blonde, young woman, who appears to me in memory with a neat, high, tight ponytail, a fresh youthful face, and a white rag in one hand. I am tall and foreign-looking, what white people call dark. I was probably ten years older than her, but I didn't look it then. She moved furniture and swept underneath. Bang bang thud bang scrape scrape scrape scrape thud scrape silent silent silence silence thud. Ear plugs don't eliminate thuds. Music doesn't cover thuds, though it may take care of the scrape, and sleeping to arrhythmia was a feat I couldn't accomplish. I was often fearful, when I lay down, that she would start just as I drifted off, and then, if she stopped any time soon, the tension of anger, the feeling that my well-being was in this callous, compulsive girl's hands, would keep me awake.

You see that she is the villain, and not I. Our apartment walls, ceilings and floors were thin, of course it's true. It was one of those East Village buildings that had been divided and subdivided into studios over the years. This was done cheaply, shoddily and we were paying, oh God, too much for it. We were young people, young unmarried people, living in New York and working our asses off just to live in New York. There were no wild bohemian weekends like you hear about in the Village in 1970 or 1949. If we had had wild bohemian weekends, how could we have worked so hard to pay our astronomical rents? Our friends in Brooklyn had it only slightly better, but people were so spread out. New York is an unsociable city in many ways. It's not what the young artist dreams of. This was not the bohemia I'd dreamed of.

We could hear everything. I could hear everything my next door neighbors did. They were a couple. One day I saw the woman, a pretty white woman with hair as dark as mine. In a year, I never saw the boyfriend. They never fought. Sometimes they laughed while they were watching TV. Sometimes they pulled out pots loudly. I could feel them having sex, the pulse of the floor under their bed, and their sweet, intimate moans.

I had a boyfriend but I couldn't sleep at his place because he was married. I never saw his place, as a matter of fact. Once and a while he could stay over because his wife traveled for business. They were young and had no children. We were all young then. On those nights, he wouldn't come over until after midnight in case she called. I liked it when he put his arms around me and we slept. I would say things to him while he made love to me. I couldn't stop talking. I felt it was necessary to say as much as possible of what I felt to him, though my feelings of tenderness, in those moments, were beyond articulation. I said yes yes I called him my baby. I told him how good it felt. I said you feel so good. He loved me but he couldn't express it. He wasn't as verbally expressive as me about his affection. He wasn't that kind of person. I thought it might scare him off to tell him that I loved him like that. So I only mouthed it with my head to the side, in our most tender moments, the full pressure of him inside of me. It seems that the tenderness, the beautiful feeling, comes from the exponential feeling of longing, the feeling that somehow, we could join even more than that, and wanting it, and feeling such exquisite, such high, sweet, reciprocation.

I loved him for his intelligence, his deftness of thought. Every story he told was made of such delicious, nuanced, imagery, like dreamlife. He couldn't tell a story without artfully laying out for you the sensual elements. I remember the story of Carpal Tunnel Mary, who had sat next to him, well, around the curve of a round table (the anti-cubicles) at the height of the web boom. There was the light sound of a computer keyboard, of wrists cracking. She breathed loudly when she wanted attention, which was often. She had a face "like a boxer" features slightly swollen and misplaced, like they'd been knocked off and put back on a bit up and off to the side. She was twenty years older than him, with a distinct joylessness, huge blob-like breasts and a resentment of his handsomeness, their proximity, a force against which she struggled daily, gave in to and bucked against. Her name wasn't Mary. She had a litany of aches and pains each with their own muffled, baby-like gurgling sounds. One day, could he massage the lump in her shoulders? Next, she wouldn't speak to him but shuffled papers with vengeance. He demonstrated the sounds, the carpal tunnel gurgle, the papers. Papers can be shuffled with vengeance. I listened.

And for my stories, he was a beautiful chorus. He made me feel listened to, and what he added made me feel like I was clever too.

One of my stories: I grew up in a small town in Michigan. I had a friend we called Bubba, who was the life-giving force, the center, of our group of friends. He didn't look like Bubba our president, not a white good ol' boy, fodder for stand-up comedians. He wasn't round and pink with the look of beer. He was tall and lean and Mexican, but the nickname was apt. All of our nicknames were apt and they all came from Bubba, even his own. His naming came from a quality of decadence, I suppose, and that he was so physically unlike what the name evokes. Irony is often a key element to the apt nickname. In my experience, all the special places I've been, all my islands of happiness, were made by one person who was capable of a large continuous flow of love. One person who lit up for everybody, and created a *group, a family* a flow of love, what it should have been, why we eventually turn to friends over family, for as long as it lasts. As soon as Bubba looked you in the eyes, he showed you his teeth. He grinned, largely, and he teased us all about our sex lives. He made us all feel attractive. I saw you eyeing Spanky last night, he said. I saw you leave the room with Matilda. And by noticing our idiosyncrasies, and naming them with love, we were all special and all acceptable in those idiosyncrasies.

Anyway, I digress. The point of this story, is that I told it to Louis and he liked it. I told Louis the story of the one and only time I saw Bubba deeply depressed. Louis was from New York, and he'd lived an artist's life, and I think there was a part of him that had wanted to be more street.

Anyway, I digress. Bubba had a Mrs. Bubba, a gorgeous blonde, with the biggest mouth of any woman I've ever known, a cursing, hateful mouth and we were all drunk all the time and Mrs. Bubba started fucking a big quiet shy hippy-type named Mellow Andy and it was rumored she took his twenty-two-year-old virginity.

Mellow Andy lived in a house with my friend named Annette, Andy and Annette were good friends. We didn't live in apartments, we lived in big houses with five bedrooms, five broke nineteen-year-olds at a time, co-ed. Yes, there was the sexual tension of roommates, but there was so much sex all over the place, it's true, we were sexually active people, that being attracted to your roommate wasn't the end of the world.

Mrs. Bubba was fucking Andy and Bubba was a wreck. Bubba wasn't lighting anyone up with his smiles. He was crouched in corners staring down into the bottom of his Mickey's Big Mouth. Bubba decided to take action. He went over to Andy and Annette's house at four o'clock in the afternoon. He brought Modelle. Modelle was named for a character in *Diner*. No one knew his real name.

Knock knock knock, a polite knock.

Hi Annette, is Andy home? Polite, too. Bubba was standing there with a baseball bat. Holding the thing to the side, like a kid asking if Andy could come out and play.

Uh, no he's not, said Annette, who knew damn well Mellow Andy was sitting in his bedroom with the lights off. Hi, Modelle, she said.

Hi, Annette, he answered, throwing up a shy wave. Okay, thanks, they said, and left.

Louis loved this story. It was symbolically about the things we had in common; we were both artists who had studied and come to be around people who had come from more money than us, from cultures very different from ours. I am from a primarily white town in Michigan, and he was from the Black and Latino Bronx, but working-class people have distinct things in common worldwide: the conspiracy of bodies in close quarters, the louder expressions of love and hate, the value of physicality and honor. My story was familiar to him. It made him laugh.

He loved my story and he gave me a chorus. "Shouldn't he be like Bubbito or something?" He changed Mellow Andy to Andy Woodnymph. He said, "So he went over to Paragon Sporting Goods…" He smiled. He knew just when to stop and let the story sit and appreciate it. When he wasn't holding me, he would just throw an ankle over mine so that we were touching. He liked my stories about Meijer's Thrifty Acres; it killed him. He said, "One of those places where you can buy a jar of olives or a couch."

Oh god, Louis.

When I met him, I had had a boyfriend. His name was Tommy. We were out watching music, this Nigerian woman who was a singer and a dancer. She had this exuberant joyfulness that I think is rare in American women, that beaming heart-love that descends upon all around. I'm sure there are others. I can't think of them right now. We are too competitive, perhaps, for that. The singer, she was in her forties, and had a commanding presence over the room. There was no doubt in her actions, her sudden moves. She had this *balance*. She would be standing and then drop, on the drum beat, in stilettos, to a position with one leg extended fully in front, squatting on one heal. Her legs swung. She seemed to be running, or moving in quantum leaps from one pose to another. What a body she had, lean and sinewy with muscular and shapely thighs. She had come out under a veil, in a dance that swept the room and one mysterious, slender, leg swinging out and then the other. When she dropped the veil, she was a very contemporary go-go girl, silver short shorts and a bikini top, like she had traveled ages. I loved that about her, very Old Country and New in one moment, just like New York. She had a shaved head. She was one of those people, I thought, who knew from a child that her place was on stage. She had no doubt. She was to be looked at and to give and receive love. She was up over the audience, leading the mood, taking us with her. There were dancers, women in the audience, who seemed to know her. A line of women stood dancing in front, of varying ability, but all at least competent in African dance, and the singer would randomly call them up one after the other. A white woman, thick and shapely, stood with her back to the audience and shook her ass. A tall, thin Black woman danced in large circles and one of her nipples was exposed.. The singer kept flirting with a white man in a suit, an overweight man who stood on his seat and danced back at her.

Tommy, my boyfriend of five months said, "The keyboard is bugging me. It's too exact."

I heard it. The keyboardist had programmed something and leaned back. He had hands resting on the sides of his instrument. It was this kind of electronic chime and it was loud and singular, one in four. Yes, very exact. Machines can never ever make music like human beings. What is the beauty, but that intangible reason to hesitate or rush to surprise to vary that any performer understands in the split seconds of improvisation that makes great players as evocative as vocalists? Any performer, musician comedian lover actor understands the power of the slight or sudden variation, the restraint, the giving over and there was the keyboard, chime two three four chime two three four. It bugged me too. I hadn't heard it and then there it was. It wouldn't go away. I resented the keyboardist. The band took a break, and I was sitting there resenting the keyboardist. Tommy went to the restroom.

While Tommy was in the restroom, I was sitting there, looking down at my hands, contemplating the keyboardist who I had not heard before, and thinking about how I would hear him the rest of the show. I was trying to think about the dancing, the marvelous balance, the sudden new angles formed by leg and torso, the flowing, the shaking. I was trying to get back where I had been emotionally, but I couldn't. I was thinking, feeling like there was something I should decide or reflect upon, I was in that state of mind. Somebody spoke to me and I couldn't make out the words.

I looked up, to see a pair of large black eyes not too far from mine. A man, Louis, was leaning a bit forward in front of my face, presenting his eyes to mine. He repeated himself. He said, "Hi, um… I just wanted to say Hi."

I had never in my life felt so attracted to a man. I had many many times thought a man was handsome, but it always felt like a cognitive decision. Up until then, I had experienced that as a lighter, decisive feeling. When I looked at Louis' face, I felt a sudden rush of blood in my body, as if the floor had dropped out in a dream. It was also emotional. It was equally intensely from the heart. When I remember it now, I remember it as coming from two parts of my body, sexual of course, and then from my heart as if my heart could reach up longingly. It was a hunger. It had to have been those eyes. Those were all I could have taken in in a moment. Louis' large, black, almond eyes.

Tommy returned. I was stuttering a response. Oh, sorry, Louis laughed, embarrassed and walked away. I didn't see him again for two years. Tommy and I broke up. He said that I was lazy and easily impressed and overly romantic. I followed the singer. I saw seven of her performances.

During those two years, of following the singer, I lost everything and got it back again. I went through a horrible depression. My cousin and I had argued. My cousin, who is white but has hair as dark as mine, said that her mother did love me like her own and that I was always oversensitive and ungrateful. She said her mother bought us the same bikes, didn't I notice, daughter and niece the same bikes, and she didn't send her, my cousin said.

She said, "She didn't send me to private school."

My cousin was a better student than I and she went to Michigan but I think she thought she could have gone to Harvard. She is a midlevel executive in Detroit. My cousin, she is married and has a big house. We fought on the phone. She said my aunt loved me. She said, "My mother sacrificed a lot for you."

She said, "No one told you to go to New York and blow everything, all that investment in your education being a slacker a…." I am not a slacker. I'm an artist. It made me think my aunt had said something to her about money. I quit speaking to them both for a long time, and those two Christmases were awful— one I spent alone I can't tell you the pain like the day my mother died. I was seven. To fend for myself. I tried to go out for dinner but I just lay there I couldn't move alone alone alone I could have died. The next Christmas I spent with a friend who didn't speak to his family either. They'd thrown him out because he is gay. We tried to go through the rituals: we got each other gifts, we ruined a ham. In the end I just wanted to get away from him so I could cry and remember my mother who had large black eyes.

I have other aunts, my mother's sisters, whom I never met. They live on the other side of the world, in the Philippines. They called me. I had never met them but they loved my mother. They said they wished they could be with me but there was no money it was better I stay there, here, in the States. I could be a doctor. They would have loved me. I remember how they sounded just like my mother. I was seven. I thought it was her. I believed she hadn't really died but had gone to the other side of the world and pretended to be one of her own sisters. I thought I was awful and she hated me and wanted to leave me. I believed that for a few years. Or I believed it and didn't at the same time.

My cousin and I finally made up. She began to weep. She felt so guilty. She knew it was all true. There was less money after I came around I changed her destiny. We are not close but we talk on the phone. I still don't know what to do at Christmas. I can't go home. I look enough like my father, and therefore my aunt, for it to look like she had two children by two different fathers, one of them colored. I know she didn't like that. It was embarrassing. It is too hard to go to her house for Christmas, but I feel my cousin would be there for me if something terrible happened, like if I ended up in the hospital. I needed to know that.

During that time, perhaps because I was so depressed, I lost my job. I just couldn't think. I had been there four years, and it was no great job. It was just some bullshit administrative stuff. I didn't even like it, but it was humiliating to get fired. I simply lost all sense of what was correct and incorrect. I would fill out a form and sit there staring at it. Was the name actually Lianna D'Angelo? Was it Leanne? De Angelo? I would look and double check and then by the time I got back to the form, forget what I had seen. I was slow. I lost things. It was humiliating. I thought I couldn't hold a job, but gradually I got better. I temped for a bit. I said to myself: this is my moment of truth. I save myself, or go off the deep end, and I decided to save myself. I gradually got better and one night in early 2001, I ran into Louis at the Singer's show. I saw his great black eyes. He said, "You probably don't remember me." I said, no, yes, I do, yes.

I learned that language is fluid it rounds corners fills crevices walks through walls. He heard everything I said. My mother my aunt. He talked to me. I cried and it was okay. It was beautiful. He could make everything okay. I was beautiful and intelligent. Everything.

I have learned a bit over time. I have learned that when we make love, we share wounds. A male friend once told me that he had a Greek lover, a woman who called his erection his wound.

Louis' life pains were like mine, huge, irreparable, at the heart of his way of being in the world.

His wife's family owned an important gallery. They didn't like him, but treated him decently because they liked to spoil their daughter. Things were beginning for him. A show in Berlin. A painting sold for $7,000.

He had to be far enough along so that they couldn't destroy him. We were careful. We would e-mail a lot. He would call me mostly when he was traveling. Once, I met him in Los Angeles, and then I would see him when she herself was out of town, or on our Friday afternoons. I cared for nothing but our Friday afternoons. After he made his way, then he could help me make mine.

By November, there were advertising campaigns referring to 9/11 about the city, perhaps this is what will characterize post-post modernism, the triumph of the age of capitalism in even our most profound reflections. If we live for another generation, they'll laugh at our vulgarity in this way, as we laugh at postwar naiveté. Anyway, I remember the picture of a young woman on the telephone, soft black and white, saying "after 9-11 we forgot why we were mad at our parents." There was this kind of discussion everywhere, exes getting back together, ex-friends calling from faraway cities, the new sense of priorities that lasted a few months.

Few talked, however, about all the people who didn't call. The fathers who disappeared on their families in 1985— you never can fully heal the abandoned child, and I know that many people spent those days in mid-September thinking, if ever there were a time, the time is now, thinking, maybe he'll call. They went through that loop one final time with the madness of loss. In our moments of vulnerability, we return to our greatest traumas. Naked, we tell our lovers about our fathers who left mothers who died the car wreck etc.

I spent those days with the friend with whom I'd spent Christmases. He didn't live far from me and so we spent those days together. He didn't feel like talking. I wanted to talk, I wanted him to hear me. I said my aunt my aunt. What I really meant was, "Louis hasn't called," but I hadn't told him about Louis because my friend would have disapproved, and so I said my aunt. That hurt too, but not so much. The phone lines are down, he said. Others got through, I said. And my aunt did call, eventually, but, I got needy. I thought I would be left to wander the streets alone. My friend Robert, he didn't want to talk. He was irritated with everything I said. I don't care what we eat who gives a fuck, he said. But I felt like if I didn't talk to him, I would disappear and so we spent a few sadomasochistic days together.

Louis called around the 17th. I didn't see him until the twenty-first. Those were bleak days. And on two of those days, the 13th and the 14th, the stomper had come in over my head just as I was drifting off, and she'd begun moving furniture to sweep. That was her way of dealing with the stress was to clean when she woke up and when she came in. She was a pretty twenty-five-year-old young woman. She should have had a boyfriend or girlfriend. I was afraid to go up and talk to her because I was afraid she'd get even louder out of anger. I had had so little sleep already and I was afraid I would go mad. I was lying there under my twisted sheets begging my raging mind to stop. I put in ear plugs but then I would just bounce and wait for daylight.

The world was on fire the southern skyline was black and we could smell it those thirty blocks up. I was wired with adrenaline and there was nothing to do but wait for Louis to call. I wanted to sleep. I was afraid to sleep. If you are like me, if you have fear of abandonment, it gives you insomnia because you feel they're going to toss you in the road while you sleep. You are a small child. You'll wake on impact, gravel in your mouth.

Louis called on the 17th. He said he was sorry. He came over on the 21st, our Friday afternoon. He kissed me. I could barely speak. I hadn't slept. While we were making love, I was losing myself losing pain, I heard her. He was making love to me holding my hands and I had almost lost myself and there she went, thud thud scrape Goddamnit dragging the bed to sweep underneath and she wouldn't stop for anything she could ruin my life, drive me mad and I was trapped there underneath her. I started to weep uncontrollably. I couldn't help it. I wanted to stop but I could barely breathe. It just happened. Louis wasn't making love to me anymore. I didn't want him to know. I hadn't wanted him to know that the way I love people is to consume them. Is to love and latch on to suck their blood to love them so much they hate me. I didn't want him to know that I eat with love. That I make them go away. But I did, I wept. I said her stomping. Her fucking stomping.

And he sat on the edge of the bed and he said, etc. and he said, that things had changed that things weren't the way they had been. We were afraid to die all of us and he had just fucked me just ten minutes before he said he wasn't coming anymore. They were leaving New York they were leaving the country they were having a baby.

He might come back. I want to marry him. New York is still alive. They said they were leaving, lots of them, and they're still here.

This isn't the bohemia I'd dreamed of.

Until It Comes to You

For some time there, I considered myself in the realm of the blessed, one of God's favored children. I was both revelrously euphoric and, I must admit, a bit callous and cruel. I thought that anyone who was not as happy as I was simply had a closed heart, was incapable of loving, that they were self-destructive and had cheated themselves out of the simplest and most thorough joy in existence. I had no tolerance for loneliness, broken heart stories, for unhappiness in general. It was their own damn fault. I let friendships slip away. I burrowed into my love, as one does. And then slowly you come up for air.

He was my first love. I started late. I was nearly thirty. Not that I was an innocent girl, that's not what I mean, but your first love is different, you're willing to die of it. I was his second and your second love you are not willing to die of. That difference drove me crazy.

Once, he tried to leave and I begged him to stay. Then, a month later, I felt like a dog after my own vomit, and to regain some semblance of power I had an affair. This time, he left easily. Bla bla bla bla bla.

And then I had no choice. I could not stay in that city any longer. To be on the same continent as him etc.

I had lived in Manila as a child, where my mother is from. I was grateful to have family on the other side of the world, as far from the site of my humiliation as possible. I had an uncle with a large house, and I invited myself to live with family I had not seen in twenty years. But my Filipino relatives welcomed me with open arms. Everyone knew why, and though I was nowhere near better quickly, I was forced to hold myself together in front of the extended family and that was a step in the right direction. I had to hold myself together and formulate plans. I went to work teaching afterschool programs in English for gifted children. The students called me "Mum," and stood up whenever speaking in class.

And then, after a while, things were all right. I began to coast.

When I could open my eyes, everything fascinated me. Imagine staring at the face of someone you have not seen in twenty years. You are not sure how you know them, but somehow an affection resurfaces. An old friend. First an emotion, and later the name. You will stare until you have the answer. Until it comes to you. I stared out the car window (for there was no walking anywhere) at the palm trees, the cigarette or fruit vendors who walked through with their wares at every stoplight. Sometimes the men, in a way I thought was beautiful, tied their t-shirts over their heads to guard their black hair from the sun. Dark colors absorb heat, my aunt reminded me. Oh yes, on a bad day, wear light colors.

Manila had changed a great deal. The traffic was unreal. The hour drive to the small town of my grandmother's birth was now three, and two of those were getting out of the city. Manila was also lit up in neon, like Las Vegas, and it was extremely Americanized, at least it seemed to me. The platinum Guess Girl stared down from billboards with her silicone pucker. Everything available in New York or LA was there Air Jordan's, Wendy's etc. etc. etc. Four supermalls, infinite endless malls sat across from each other in our section of the city.

Filipinos are great storytellers. Filipinos, when they speak English well, as most of the educated and many of the uneducated, do, speaks it beautifully. A poetic, eloquent English. Huge vocabularies and a creativity in using them, a love for language play, a boldness and openness.

A culture which functions on reciprocity creates individuals who value every connection they can make. A culture which functions on nepotism creates individuals who value every connection they can make.

A culture which functions on reciprocity creates individuals who value every connection they can make. Many more people made gestures of friendship toward me than ever before. They greet you with their arms spread. I also had many little cousins and cousins' children in the family, and there was always one around to cuddle and tease. Imagine the relief I felt.

I had been living in New York for ten years. I said to myself: New York has passion but no love. And I wished I had someone to share this observation with, and I missed him, and made note of the fact that it was in passing. I had missed him, but in passing.

I met Marivi after I had been there for six months, which was perfect timing. If I had met her earlier, I would not have had the confidence to befriend her. After six months, I forgot I was wretched. I have never in my life, aside from my own sister, met anyone whose system of reference so coincided with my own. Not after years of cultivating relationships, friendship, the love of my life, had I ever built such commonality. She was a Filipino-American, born and raised in New York, who had moved to Manila, her first visit, three years previously.

It was not just the fact of our two families' immigrations, or the dialects of New York, the joy in making note of quirks of Filipino English or imitating Long Island Jews. We even both had punk rock phases, and hip-hop phases and listed off obscure bands from these eras, we shrieked at the lyrics we could summon from memory.

We shared favorite works: I mentioned *Notes from the Underground* and Rivi, as we called her for short, she got up to pace, to enact the scene in which the narrator despises his companions, and paces, fuming on the other side of the room, desperate for their attention.

It was the David Lynch show, though, that we kept going back to. She had seen every bit of *Twin Peaks,* every episode and I had only seen the first episode and the prequel. She said your entire perception changes as it moves along. And I wouldn't let her explain why, as someday I would finish it. But she said to me, "You feel you know what happened?" Yes, I said. "Well, you don't," and she laughed. "But," she said— "it began to fail." Lynch was less involved, it seemed. It grew sentimental, a horrible weakness, sentimentality.

The prequel— when the father morphed into Bob. Yes, she said, four or five shots of the father and then one of Bob. We discussed it all in amazement, the adrenaline, the fear, Lynch could put in your veins. No one does fear or panic like he does. The flashes of things we see and think we see. Yes, remember, the first episode. The mother staring into space and remembering, recounting endlessly, hour after hour, until finally Bob's face arises, flashes for that split second between the bed posts.

How many episodes of our lives do we scour for clues hoping the answer will come, and how often does it come? Why did he? Why did I? Why must? Never, it never comes. Seldom to Never.

That was ours, *Twin Peaks*. I began to believe that Rivi was the best thing I ever had. A friend, you just may have her forever. And an intense friendship, it is much like a romance. You revel and adore.

We thought we were funny. We thought we were deliciously witty. Although, I must admit, we were not those clever people who are patient for the right moment, who have impeccable timing. Who only say what has never been said before, what is sure to raise waves of laughter. Wits of patience and precision. Naw, we said whatever popped into our head, and sometimes we drove things that worked into the ground. There are advantages to this method as well. We were always comfortable. There was no shame in failure. And it was clearly our goal to always be laughing together. And I do not think that the constant attempt diminishes the quantity of magic moments. The perfect timing, the absurd image, the great irony. We developed our own language in about eleven days. We loved to curse. We cursed blue storms. We felt that this sacrilege was our own.

Rivi introduced me to her circle of friends, a tight knit group of artsy-fartsy bohemian types. About half of them were what was called 'Balikbayan' which means something like 'Homecoming.' This phenomenon, a product of American immigrant culture, this mutation of ex-patriotism, it inspires that feeling of longing, unity. Filipinos who had been raised in the West— some were there by choice, and some through an intense family loyalty which made them wistful. There was a girl who was only eighteen from San Francisco, who had come to study. She was a tremendous dancer and the one truly fluent Tagalog-speaker of the *Balikbayans*. Another guy from SF who had several body piercings and tattoos. A guy from LA, a couple from Hawaii and a girl who had been raised in Australia. Other members of the circle were bohemians for other reasons, artists, intellectuals, many of them gay. There was a white guy from London and several people who worked in the music industry.

It was much more like my small hometown in Michigan than New York, in the sense that we would see the same people night after night. We developed a closeness which is difficult to maintain in New York. We hung out at this place called Blue, drinking, and Rivi and I did elaborate postmortems after every night out.

She worked freelance in production and had weeks off at a time and since I taught at an after-school program, we were free to go out nightly. Neither of us drove, so we had to depend on other friends to collect us. They were always young men, mostly people who Rivi had met through production work and they usually had crushes on her. Rivi was very pretty. There was something very feline about her. She was petite and had huge eyes and wore her hair piled on the back of her head in a way that gave her the line of a cat, that was elegant. I am a tall person, by Filipino standards especially, and I'm sure we made a curious pair running about Manila with me towering over her.

When I first met Max, I did not think anything of him. He and Rivi picked me up and we were supposed to go to a play in a distant part of the city. We were completely unrealistic about the traffic and halfway there came to a complete standstill with no end in sight. Max did not laugh at our jokes, not one, and we were on that night. And it was not because we were speaking that language only we understood— we had adjusted that for him, but because he simply did not seem to appreciate a bit of it. I thought he was uptight. He was tall and skinny, as tall as myself. And he wore his hair parted in the middle and smoothed down, and had a pencil mustache. He also wore a loose white peasant shirt. There was something about him which was of another era. When he got out for cigarettes, leaving the car smack dab there in the middle of the roadway, I whispered to Rivi that he looked like a musketeer.

Of course, you understand by now that he will come to play a significant part in this story. We finally pulled off, when the gridlock broke, which was halfway through the play, into an empty rock and roll bar. We ordered beers. It was the height of the rainy season and the rain started coming down in sheets.

Rivi and I went on amusing ourselves. She told us about seeing a flamenco performance, reenacting the way the dancers breathe during pauses. Max was distracted. He began to irritate me. He didn't seem to be listening at all, and then he was screwed up tightly, positively school marmish. He sat with his back rod straight, and his lips were actually pursed. And so, I figured if he was going to pretend we were not there, I, at least, would do likewise, and I launched our favorite schtick, the *we are American Urbanites* schtick. Our conspiracy. In a couple of minutes we were diagramming the sentence *Where the motherfucker at?* Max was not a Balikbayan and he would not be able to share in this.

Then Rivi went to the bathroom and Max laid his hand on the table. He had very long slim, almost feminine fingers and I liked them and I had to admit to myself that he irritated me because I was attracted to him and felt no reciprocation. It also occurred to me, that he looked, not like a musketeer but like a nineteenth century revolutionary, like the *ilustrados*, the educated of the Spanish colonial era, often sent to Europe to study, who wrote deathly lonely, poetic letters home and came back to write anti-colonial treatise, some titled in Latin.

I nicknamed him "Apolinario" in my mind, thinking I would tell him later, although I wasn't sure who Apolinario was. I liked the sound of the name. I vaguely remembered it applied to some national hero who might be obscure enough for me to appear knowledgeable. I remembered the story of some general directing the revolution from his death bed. And that sickliness, that languorous tragedy— it all seemed appropriate to Max.

And then Max, after a silence which was embarrassingly long to myself and perfectly natural to him, asked me what I did for a living. And then he asked me what I was reading, a question which furthered my attraction, and then I asked him, and he said, I swear on my mother, Rousseau. I decided that Max was a tortured genius, and he turned me on.

Rivi returned from the bathroom. We ordered the most delicious garlic mushrooms before God. And Max, he brought it up, began a conversation comparing Manila to New York, which he had visited on two occasions. I was down on New York. The last two months before I left were perhaps the worst of my life. Not only was I in the throes of depression, but because I was leaving, as is natural, I suppose, as is usually the case, my friends began to withdraw from me.

They leave us as soon as we know they want to; is that not the case?

So I packed up my apartment by myself and lugged overstuffed luggage to the airport in the middle of the night. It took two trips up and down my four flights of stairs. That fucking place. And when I got to

Manila my entire extended family was there. I mean, twelve cousins, eight cousins' children etc. etc. They all came to see me within a day of my arrival, and then I met Rivi and this crowd of people. And I felt such a profound relief.

Rivi missed New York and counted the days for her return. She was tired of her scene being small. She missed New York's Independent Film Industry, and knowing, with such facility, people from all over the world.

I was ranting about New York, I must say. I became emotional. I said it was fucking heartless and that is supposed to be cool. I said no one gives a shit. I said they step over you. Max said, but don't you see, don't you see, that's better. People leave you alone. They don't judge you.

I could see that he felt persecuted as I felt abandoned and I could see that he had never— he had never been that lonely. He had no idea what it was to feel that if you fell off the face of the earth no one would notice.

"Once I took myself to the hospital for food poisoning. Did you ever take *yourself* to the hospital. I had to wait...." My voice began wavering and I stopped. I was embarrassed.

"But Eva," Rivi said. I will call myself Eva. "How hungry are people here? How hard do poor people work for people with money, right in their houses? How heartless is that? The class exploitation," she said, referring to the extensive system of servants even people in the middle class had. Yes, Max said. Yes, that is the point. I could not answer.

And what could come between us, I saw it all then. Sometimes you can see in a flash, the nature of a relationship. I could see that he was a desperate man. That the disinterest I made note of earlier was clearly the simplest fear. That he could love Rivi as well as myself, or many other girls, any remotely intellectual woman who would pay him mind. Rivi would not. Me, I was in the mood for something impossible. I could see that a man like that would take anything. He would cower more as one's irritation increased. My capacity for cruelty would expand to his capacity to withstand it. This would prove his theories about persecution.

It became impossible to continue the New York-Manila conversation as we were, all three of us upset, and nowhere near empathizing the least bit with anyone else's point of view. We stabbed the last mushrooms with tooth picks, leaving one in the center, the piece of shame— and went to find the others at Blue.

The front of the bar was painted with this wonderful impure shade, blue with a breath of red, toward violet on the color wheel. The tables were a deep brown, cherry-like, although it was not cherry. There was something heavy, and cool about the place. It was my favorite. They played funk.

Wendy was there, the teenage dancer from San Francisco and she was dancing. She was tiny and cute and for that reason brings up maternal feelings, made us feel liked, had a bold smile. Actually, she was this incredible combination of cute and sultry at the same time. She wore gowns, velveteen, or silk, and her hair was always elaborate, arranged ringlets, piled in back, braids, beads. She had killer black heavy eyebrows and sometimes she threw glitter over her nose like freckles. She had a high-pitched, feminine voice, and yet she could be scathing when on the defensive. I had teased her about something and she called me a human table cloth. I looked down at my shirt, I was a human table cloth and I had trouble enjoying the rest of the evening, because I knew myself I had overstepped a line when I teased her. And as coifed and arranged as she was— her dancing was completely unselfconscious. It was athletic and graceful, light as a gymnast.

Tina was also there, the Australian girl. She was the queen of those comments which are not extreme enough to be insults, and so cutting in their subtlety. *My, those shoes are sexy* to the girl who now worries that her shoes are whorish, or *you're getting fat, just kidding*. She was at the end of the long table where our friends sat, and there was a seat open next to her, and two at the opposite end. Marivi, whose instincts are always on, she took the torturous space next to Tina and let Max and I place ourselves together.

We turned to watch Wendy for a moment, then watched people watching Wendy, a couple, the girl leading her boyfriend away by the elbow, the waiters who became absorbed, forgot their customers, and started awake to their summons. I looked for Max's eyes, but he sat stiffly next to me with his hands folded between his knees. I could almost feel the arid cracking of his bones. I looked for Rivi's eyes but she was talking to Tina and Tina's boyfriend, a DJ with hair that stood up in front like a flame.

Max's back began to curve over as if there were something wrong with his stomach. I asked him about his work, which carried the vague name of "consultancy." He explained it to me and I did not understand his answer. I waited for him to make an effort in the conversation and he did not. I turned to the other side, looking for someone else to talk to. Dante was there, who was purportedly asexual, which I had trouble believing. We spoke for a moment. Then, I turned to include Max, and told the stories of my attempts at Tagalog. The way I'd asked my cousin's son *Nose years you now?* and the time I tried to tell the maid I was not going to eat and said instead that I had not yet eaten.

Max laughed, for the first time that evening, as I recall, and feeling something had changed, I turned back to him. When you meet someone you can talk to— how magic we are in those first few conversations when we tell all our best. I told him about my sense of Manila, its hyper Americana and he said that that was observant of me. He spoke of "collecting data" verses "generating ideas." He said you can't speak in abstraction in Tagalog and I argued that that was untrue, that it was simply that he had studied in English, had never even made the attempt in Tagalog, and he laughed that I was the *Amerikana* and how would I know? He accused me of romanticizing. He said he would give anything to leave, which made me grow conscious of my citizenship, like it was a big wad of money.

It was not so much the content of the conversation which made me feel as if I had completely misjudged him— but a confidence which had been missing the previous hours. He did something I thought was clever. He spoke more and more quietly until I positively had to press my ear to his mouth. I was waiting for him to kiss me. I began, already, to formulate the post-mortem for Rivi.

She gazed directly from across the table, shaking her head, titling the episode "You won't believe this shit." She turned back to speak to Tina. It was easy for us to communicate.

Somebody ordered shots and we threw them back, wincing. Max said he'd raised himself. He said don't let them fool you into thinking they give a shit. He told the one about the cop who said, "Yes, my brother toyed with narcotics too," and let him go. He said it must have been the cop himself.

I told him that he looked like a nineteenth century revolutionary and that I'd named him Apolinario. He didn't know how to take it. He explained that Apolinario was the man's first name, Apolinario Mabini. He was working class, came up through the ranks, and lost the use of his legs. They called him the Sublime Paralytic, and he wrote important texts of the revolution. Max said that they had killed him, his fellow-officers, his supposed *kumpadres*. I asked why but Max did not know. I asked for the name of the one who directed the revolution from his death bed, who was that, and Max did not know what I was talking about. I asked the whole table. I asked Dante and yelled down to Rivi and Tina, then Wendy who was studying history at the time. No one knew what I was talking about. They paused, squinting and went back to their respective conversations.

Max began to positively mumble. I thought about how much we'd drunk. I looked up to see Rivi laughing, with her hand on Tina's forearm. And then I glanced up again a moment later, and she had been watching me. She was not trying to tell me something, but watching me, figuring something, and then she leaned to speak to Tina.

It occurred to me that all of these people were Rivi's friends and not mine. That hers was the only phone number I had, and that if she had not organized rides for me night after night, I would have been stuck at my uncle's house, holding myself together as I'd done months before.

The party began to dissipate. Dante left us for Freddie the owner, who always had the same table on the patio, and had a habit of asking people how old they were and telling them they looked younger. Wendy took a contingent to a club. Some went to get high, and Rivi and Max and I resituated to a small, round table.

Max was weaving around a bit from the hips up, and his black eyes focused obliquely down the street. I was worried about him driving home.

I explained to Rivi the whole Apolinario thing and she agreed that yes, Max was something of another time. What do you use in your hair? she asked. Gel? Saliva? She licked her hand. When he laughed, his timing was off. Rivi was smiling. I laughed in one ironic breath, and as if that were the signal, the starter's gun, then he laughed in a bark, and leaned over, clutching his stomach. My eyes widened. I looked for Rivi's but she was watching him.

Max said something which was positively a gurgle, like a baby eating. What, we asked, what what? And after several attempts, we were able to decipher: "They want to know about the nineteenth century mind."

And then, Max, oh, it's positively embarrassing the way he would clutch himself. I worried for his bowels. Then he sat up suddenly. His head moved, birdlike from one angle to another. Then it was as if he were watching fireworks, eyes darting this way and that within a confined radius, reacting, every few beats, to the light, starting back, jumping away.

We watched him. I was extremely worried about how we would get home. Taxis are notoriously unsafe in Manila, especially for one like myself, my Tagalog was not passable. I was obviously not from here. Tourists got mugged, and the rich.

Rivi was still trying to speak to Max. I had resigned myself to his insanity.

"The sky looks good tonight, right?" she asked. She said it a few times.

I wanted to communicate with her, and I was not quite sure how lucid Max was, what he understood of what we said. So I asked her this: "Remember Bob's disease from *Twin Peaks?* I think it's here with us." He was the one who lived in the basement of the hospital. And everyone who came into contact with him contracted his disease. They spoke a pearl of wisdom here and there, and nonsense everywhere else.

"Yes, they become like these oracles. Max, did you see *Twin Peaks?*" I cringed.

I had brought up the whole thing. It was my fault. Yes, my predictions were right. I was cruel. One could see that Max suffered horribly, and yet, it made me laugh. I had wanted him and he was insane and it was quite a story, really.

"Max," she said again, "Did you see *Twin Peaks?*" Max laughed in that same sudden moan.

Then he gurgled again and again and finally, "But don't you see?" came out.

I was trying to catch Rivi's eyes. See that she understood. But she was still trying to make conversation with Max.

Finally, he turned to me and without gurgles, boldly and frankly, he spoke a full, clear phrase in Tagalog. All I understood was 'they' and that it was in future tense.

Then I knew he could not be near lucid. I said to Rivi, "Now I know he's gone because he knows I don't know what he's saying." And then we threw up our hands, shook our heads at the sky. In my mind there was the eternal struggle between a ridiculous politeness. *Max you are way too fucked up to drive.* And the gamble on a taxi. Yes, people get held at gun point. Yes, it happened to people I knew.

I insisted we should take a taxi. I insisted we make him take the taxi with us. And then Max, turned to me again, with that owl-like stiffness. His black eyes— it was as if he had no pupils. He looked in my general direction and saw something completely unrelated to me. He spoke, I swear to God, he said something in Hindi.

It gave me the creeps. I said, can we go? We paid the bill, and lifted him by each elbow. One on each side. We're taking a taxi, I explained. My car, he said.

We got in the taxi. Rivi first, Max in the middle. As ridiculous as it was, it was Max's presence which I felt would keep us safe from the crap shoot with drivers.

My car, he said. It's okay, I said. It's okay, baby. You can get your car tomorrow. I spoke with a mocking sweet sexiness. I did it for entertainment, for Rivi's sake. The driver thought we were hookers trying to roll Max.

"No, I can't leave my car," he said.

"Max, you are far too," and I said, "*drunk*, to drive."

"No, I can't leave my car." He started awake. Rivi asked him if he was sure. She held him firmly by the wrist and looked him in the eye and he looked back, and swallowed. Yes, he was sure. And the cab driver stopped, a block from Blue, and we watched Max walk with effort back to his car. It was then that I was certain he could control it.

Rivi told the driver in Tagalog where to go. She was sitting forward in the seat peering at the road. I was still quite helpless in Manila, as far as navigating was concerned, and if I had been alone he could have driven me anywhere. I wanted to start our post-mortem immediately.

"Max…" I said, and Rivi held up her hand for me to be quiet. She scooched further forward in the seat, and said to the driver, in a simple Tagalog, again, which she only spoke when absolutely necessary, "Where are you going?" And then he explained that this route would circumvent traffic. She stayed scooched and watching the roadway. And the whole evening…. how could I wait to talk about it?

"Max, man, did you know how into him…." and she gave me the sternest look she had ever given me. A firm and angry meeting of the eyes. I knew, yes, then that she did not want the driver to hear us speaking English. But it was painful that she could give me that sort of look at all. I felt huge and useless. A gross appendage of flesh, detrimental, in fact, dangerous.

We drove on in silence. I watched Manila without its vendors. It was still lit up in neon, these few hours in the middle of the night before people would begin walking the roads begging or selling flowers and peanuts and fruit to cars stuck in traffic. It took us about twenty minutes to traverse the distance which had taken us hours earlier in the evening. We stopped at my uncle's house first and I got out, kissing Rivi on the cheek. She kept her eyes on the road, with that same, narrowed, concentrating look.

I rang the bell and the guards let me in, smiling in that way reserved for the family black sheep, the knowledge that somehow my decadence aligned me more with them. We shared a secret. There was threat in their smiles.

The driver. He slowed down, and asked Rivi for a cigarette. He thought we were hookers.

Does everyone know things only in passing? I took the hair to Eveline. I said Eveline, is this a red hair or a brown hair? That's a red hair isn't it, a red fucking hair. And the look she gave me… and I could never face her after that. And still I begged. You don't remember what it's like down there. You have no sympathy. And yet there is freedom in being a bastard.

Yes, a defeated human being. Yes, it was positively excruciating to watch his self-consciousness, even his walk. The look of overexposed film or the red eyes. They tell you you shouldn't. They hold themselves in a certain way, like they don't want to shit, and then tell you you should not.

Isa. Dalawa. Takbo.

Where were you?

I'll change.

I'll

Flesh and Blood

I write in two ways. The one I have not used as much of late is a very slow-going method in which my ideas come to me in moments of distraction, like satisfying dreams. Actually, better I should say, they're very slow-going at first, and then sudden, flies in the fist. I have always thought of this as the real way to write, and I think that the stories I've written in this way tend to be better. The second method I've used, which I've used more in the past few years, with regret, is faster, and involves a bit more of my leading, and forcing, and less of my feeling like a vessel. Sometimes I feel quite satisfied with my prose in this method. Sometimes it's even stronger, but the events of the stories feel less creative and surprising, and it doesn't quite feel real. At times, the emotions of the second method seem off to me. Also, that this particular Lara Stapleton aspires to a bit of pity in the wrong moments. I don't mean self-pity in narrators, that can be interesting, but I mean asking the readers for sorrow in moments that are not moving enough, not that unique to human suffering. The continuum of human empathy is off.

I have come to accept this second method. I don't know if it will ever feel as good as the first, but I'm coming to enjoy the production and even the finished stories. I got used to it in the era of constant distraction. It was sometimes all I had. I just no longer had a week to walk quietly by myself anymore, and I've just stuck with it for some reason, even though now I do have that solitude, an excessive amount of it.

Part of my acceptance comes from reading Roberto Bolaño's short stories recently. I identify with his feeling of landlessness, his being both Chilean and Mexican, having immigrated as a youth, then morbidly betrayed by his homeland, imprisoned during a visit as a young adult because his accent made him suspect in the authoritarian times. So, neither of these countries are his, he feels, and his "homeland is the

Spanish language." His stories are set everywhere, in Mexico City, with its fierce young intellectuals, in Barcelona and St. Petersburg. He uses scenes from dreams and films, pornos, and his narratives can be like meandering conversation, an overheard snippet, a sudden leap to somewhere else without justification.

I love his structures. They're so surprising, and after struggling with what are proper subjects and explorations, I felt very free after reading his intent bohemia.

People often interpret bohemia to mean a recklessness of the body, booze and promiscuity. That can be part of it, but not necessarily, and that's not what I mean, myself, when I say "intent bohemia." I mean that an artist is an artist day and night, and that the life of a writer, reading, for example, and dreaming, and staring at the river waiting for an idea, is full of actions that can be written about like fishing or living through a car crash. Elena Ferrante is another writer who has captured this well, I think.

I compose this during the COVID-19 pandemic and our long-term quarantine. I have been very fortunate to be teaching on-line, and though this isolation is hard for nearly every single person, I think it is less difficult for a writer. I have had the time to get up and write for three or four hours, five or even seven days a week, and that has been very much the work I enjoy. It's been a productive time, especially now that I have some time off between semesters. I am interrupted by nothing, not by Tommy, not by my sister, and not by my students.

I've also had the good fortune of a great deal of time to work on who I want to be as a human being, and I've discovered something magical and that is that I can control my emotions much more than I had believed in the past. I can create emotions in my body through concentration. These are very vague senses of these emotions, they are not strong feelings, but thin layers of them. Yet I have begun to have the sense that with time and effort, I will be fully in control of these feelings. I'll be able to turn them up and down as if with a volume button.

I believe the seeds of this are from seeing the poet Elizabeth Alexander speak before the closing. In the after-reading discussion, she spoke on the difference in writing in various forms. She made a motion indicating that her poems came somewhere from the womb or torso.

She gestured with a sweep from the guts up toward the mouth, a gesture of expression. And she then said that her essays come from her brain, the logical part, I suppose she meant, and now with an arc of the hands from behind the eyes and then again toward the mouth, this time a motion down.

The creative spirit, for me, words on a page, come from the base of the skull, a bit to the right. I also write poems and essays, though not often, and I cannot tell if different forms come from different parts of my body, but I do know that the creative spark is found in the right, back, portion of my brain toward where the skull curves into the neck. And then, after I contemplated this a few months back, I realized, that not just my work, but my emotions have certain bases in the body.

Peace, or at least contentment, is some center part of the cranium. I can concentrate on this inner section, create a pressure cerebrally, and I can feel the very mist of a cool sensation, I'm releasing some chemical. Love is in my chest, a pressing slightly center left that gives me an urge to put my hands there. Again, these are ghost feelings, not the strong sensation that one has from organic life experience, but I can tend and grow them. Further back in the brain, lower toward the top of the spine, is the seed of boisterous laughter.

Among these emotions that now seem accessible to me, the vaguest, and perhaps the most beneficial, is gratitude. Gratitude is the most generalized of the emotions with which I've been experimenting. I cannot tell you from where exactly in the body it comes, except that it's upper body, more chest than brain, but somewhat of both. I can find it sometimes, that thin layer, and I feel that if I find it more precisely, it will be the key to happiness, and that I will be generally happy. This is probably the most important of all. Perhaps it combines many of the others, or is a result of many of the others, or perhaps the base of the others. This is especially true in this time of the pandemic, which has been unusually positive and optimistic for me, though dark for others.

There were just a couple of times that the emotion was more intense, stronger than that thin layer. This is what convinces me I will soon have much more control. There were days where I sent jolts of happiness through the left cephalic vein, which stretches from the collarbone to the elbow. It's funny that it is specifically my left and not my right, but it is. On these days, I have missed Tommy because, of course, I wanted to share this elation with him, and I missed my sister, but truth is, I don't think I could have learned as much as I've learned if I had been speaking to the two of them. When the emotion is intense, and I feel very high, it is with a touch of longing, which is a truly exquisite combination of emotions, something like what we feel when we come upon art that astounds us.

Perhaps if I had mastered these phenomena earlier, like before Tommy and I even got together, or in our early days, we wouldn't have broken up. Truth is, I'm not really feeling our breakup yet because these sensations are so exhilarating, but I imagine I will sometime soon. I miss him, but it is a distant, curious feeling, like hearing the story of someone else's life.

What I miss about Tommy is his gentleness. Imagine the moment in which a person sets down a glass. I remember being struck by that on our first date. Tommy is a big, physically powerful person. He continually has the look of someone too big for the furniture, holding himself across chest. This is an irony for a man who is fundamentally a sensitive type. He has poise in his voice, though, something very precise. It is deep and sonorous, with a cadence of purposeful calm. He pauses in conversation with his mouth shaped for what's coming, he holds it there a moment, eyes narrowed. He lets what he said last sink in, a masterful instinct for the suspense of good conversation. I think of a paternal newscaster, of a man expressing tender concern to his adult daughter. I remember his setting down a wine class, that awareness of delicacy inside his big, meaty hands. He also has a large laugh, laughter that shakes him, but when he sets down a glass, it is with that gentle precision that showed there and in his voice.

We only made it through seven months of the pandemic, and we had only been together a year before that, but he was the love of my life. I'm aware of this, though I'm watching it all from a distance. This is perhaps why it hasn't hit me yet, it's too big to process all at once. It will creep up on me, I imagine. I imagine that one day I'll be sitting with my breakfast, and then I'll remember, I'll remember his two fingers walking around the back of my head and pulling me toward him, and a longing will come to me, an ache, a whole-body wound. I can feel its suggestion. I can sometimes feel this other wounded body inside of mine, but it has not overtaken me, and I've been enjoying my experiments with emotion.

Our break-up happened the way I might have expected it to happen. He sat me down at the round kitchen table, where I would write after he'd gone to work. He took my one hand in two of his, and I'm embarrassed to say, I thought he was proposing. I was scared, and I felt like yanking my hand from his, like a girls' clap game. I would say my adrenaline was at top speed, and his was calming, in spite of what he was doing. I didn't rip my hand from his. I learned as we were dating to resist the urges to bolt that visit me.

What he said was cliché, and I hate to recount it but feel I should. He loved me, but that love had shifted. He didn't see us getting married, so what was the point? His feelings had become mostly platonic and though he knew that would hurt me, I deserved someone that was sure. My hand grew sweaty, and he was rubbing the back of it, and it felt like a ridiculous false comfort, like he was holding my hand with disdain. I had the feeling his kindness was false, that a man like him wants to appear to the world as a *good* person. Look how good he was, running his fat fingers over the veins in the back of my hand and I knew that he had known all along. He had suggested we live together as the quarantine began. He had been promising a future, and walking his fingers around my head.

So, I pressed him for more. I said, "There is not no reason. You thought you could love me, and then you knew you couldn't," and the way he turned his head, and shaped his mouth for the words to come, as he always does, I knew that even that wasn't true. He had known all along he couldn't love me. There must have been a bit of rot in his gut, resting there because he knew full well it was all a lie. He had been so creative with his affection, his sudden small bottle of oil, his birthday card that said, "best," and "only." He could do these things because he wasn't really risking anything. He was just experimenting, getting over his last and preparing for his life partner. And there was my sweaty hand between his two, his disdainful pats and icky swirls.

We don't have the right chemistry, he said.

But there's a reason, I said, tell me.

And his contemplative pauses, and something vague again, then finally, he said, "When I first met you, and saw you didn't cook very much though you're good at it, and you sometimes forget to buy gifts, I thought it was feminist. I thought you were making a statement to the world about your role. You had this independence I wanted, too. Sometimes I care too much what people think." I agreed. His long days at work: the more his boss ignored him, the longer he stayed. "But now, I see, it's a coldness. You just have this coldness, and you say it's to write, but no. Lots of times you say you're going to write, but you're on Instagram and you won't talk to me. You do that for a whole weekend. It's odd. Those people aren't really your friends." I knew he truly felt this, when it finally came out, but I knew there was more. I asked for more, I asked a few times, but he wouldn't say. The last thing he did say in that conversation was that he wished the best for me, and my hand was still there between his two, sitting there like meat going bad.

He packed a suitcase, put that silly light blue mask over his face, and got in an Uber to go stay with his cousin. He kept paying rent, he wanted out badly enough that he went somewhere else but payed his half of our rent out of his nice-guy guilt. I did feel somewhat badly for a couple of weeks, but not really that much. I wrote three stories during this pandemic, and I've been able to wake up every day and write about my dreams, the most delicious thing in the world.

Truth is, I suspect that Tommy felt what a lot of so-called forward-thinking men experience, a discomfort with my priorities, my being an artist interrupting the attention he thought he deserved.

My writing now, comes from memories. Before, I used to really enjoy going to various places around the city where I could find stillness. I'd just people-watch at Prospect Park, or ride the Staten Island Ferry, and after a while, a feeling of profundity would come, a distillation. I would go home with a nugget based on something I saw, scrawled in a small notebook, and I'd hold that nugget overnight, reminding myself occasionally throughout the evening, and it felt so like that satisfying dream, like a message with answers to burning questions had come just for me.

Writing from memory now, my stories are more contemplative, less based in events. I'm enjoying this, but if I can, after I complete the story I'm working on, which is very much of this style, I want to go back to something more plot-based, something more flesh and blood.

I broke the back of this particular story on one of the happiest nights of my life. I have been working on it very slowly, very, very slowly. It's only eight pages so far, but I've been on it for months. I have the feeling there is another story beneath this one that will come to me in the old way, a visitation, about people I do not yet know, and events nothing like what I've experienced.

One of the happiest nights of my life was a couple of months into the pandemic. We had learned a little bit more about the disease by then, and so, we decided it was okay to have a couple of friends over on my birthday if we sat outside. We drank wine on my stoop. We're friends with this lesbian couple, Lynn and Larilyn, two Filipino-Americans. Things had been a little stale between Tommy and me, I could feel his irritation. He always did the right thing, always washed the dishes if I cooked, and asked about my day, but our relationship began to lack things that had been there before, his ankle tossed over mine, his sudden boisterous laughter. One day, when I asked about dinner *again,* he shrugged as if I shouldn't have asked. This wasn't his way, he was always pleasant. So, the shift stood out to me.

But the night my friends came over, something opened, and my brain felt cool and lifted. The three of us together are Lara, Lynn and Lar-i-lynn. Ha ha ha. We have a repertoire of jokes about this, and we tell every new person we cross paths with about our Voltron name, and then there's the bit about how they're a couple but Lynn and I are Larilyn's parents. On our stoop it turned into a bit about Tommy's three wives, two of whom refuse to have sex with him. I got to say a bit about how I was relieved by that, but that I had seen Larilyn eyeing his ass. Our landlords came out with a bottle of wine, excited for company themselves, I think, and we chatted about the evolution of the neighborhood. They had lived there thirty years.

I had been trying to write the story, and trying to write the story, and I felt myself dissolve a bit, become aware of my particles floating in other particles and yet at the same time I felt my lungs expanding, joy is in the lungs, and Tommy had just stood up and turned around and showed his ass to Larilyn. He stood there for a moment, twitching from side to side. She grew tall with a deep breath, she was to feign disapproval, properly working within the rhythm of the scene, and I watched her whole face pucker, then the cascade of laughter.

I held her lift and burst in my mind. It sat with me, and as our communion-on-the-stoop continued, something crystalized for my story. What if that lift and pause, that moment before something happens, were sad and not joyous? What if it were standing on one side of a door having to do something awful, and breathing in and bracing oneself, and the growing taller was with fear, and this fear lingered? This lingering after the preparation breath broke my story. It was that thing, that moment that interested me enough that it could sit in my mind while the rest gathered around it. I would enjoy it. I had this secret all to myself while we laughed on the stoop. And Tommy and I fell asleep smirking and the next day we walked in the park. I had so much. I had the tale resting in my mind. I had the Voltron of my friends, and I was in love. This is the last time I remember our relationship being that good.

There is something I haven't told you yet. I waited a long time to tell Tommy, too. I didn't tell him until we moved in together, and although he said the things he felt right, "Oh, it's probably nothing. Oh, that happens to people all the time, you're just noticing it now," I recall now that he was making those same icky swirls and pats on the back of my hand. He also asked me how long it had been going on, and why I didn't tell him sooner, and as I recall it now, very clearly, I can see the retreat in his eyes betraying that incessant kindly man voice. "Don't worry," he said. "I think it's your fear driving it. You'll forget about this soon."

It started with printed words. By January, I started misperceiving entire printed sentences. I saw my own name printed across the bottom of a shampoo bottle, where it directs purchasers to "Discover strength, shine and softness." Instead, I read, "Discover, stapleton, lara and softness."

In the beginning, I would see the first few letters of a word, and mistakenly assume its end. At first, it was simply varying word forms, "sequential" instead of "sequence." Who would worry about that? I reminded myself not to read too fast.

Then it was unrelated words with the same beginnings, "panther" instead of "pander." "Vendor" instead of "Venn Diagram." Again, an issue of reading too fast.

Then I saw my name across the plastic. I looked once; it was clear as day, "stapleton, lara," and then I looked again, and it said "strength, shine and softness." "Arrowroot flour" became "agonizing floor." I also saw words that didn't exist, "avove," "skartly."

Adult onset dyslexia? I joked to myself and once I even told my sister Marta on the phone.

Then, one day, I saw a denim shirt bolt across our fire escape, as if there were a road there, and a thief had shot from one end to the other. But we're on the second floor. And in an instant, I saw that it was a small, black bird. This is when I decided to tell Tommy. Swirl, pat, swirl, pat. This is what he wouldn't say as he told me he was leaving, that I scared him. I had forgotten this part. I am only remembering now.

It would be nice if I were visited by the characters in my stories with the clarity of that denim shirt. As of now, it is only thin layers, mists of their presence, but I think it will come eventually.

My sister and I had been close. Who else is born of the same strange tale of migration and rot? And we laughed about it.

They tell you must sit with a stern listener, that this firm lady will guide you to face yourself and do better as you blame the world, this stern lady who asks why you did this or that according to the theories of her graduate study. These ladies keep you angry. They make you stare at haunting basements and they immerse you in the infinite longing of a child. Why should I feel the infinite longing of a child? When I feel my particles floating in the particles of the air, of my city block, of the loving people of the world, why should it be with terrible longing? Why shouldn't I do so with the love I've built of my warm heart, my awareness of my chest, center left? When I dissolve, why shouldn't it be with my love radiating from my wishes, and not the world-size longing of a wounded child?

So, my sister and I, we shared dark humor. Rotten food: funny. Snarling tempers: funny. She called the week after Tommy left, but she did not care that he had left.

I had no idea she'd been keeping score, that in the previous year, I had called three days after her birthday. Apparently, I'd done this two years in a row. And it's true I take a long time to call back sometimes. But the kicker, the thing she couldn't forgive, is that I hadn't called her after her miscarriage. She left me two messages. The first I believe I missed, the second, I do recall, but I thought she was just letting me know. She's married, after all, and I trust they share that disappointment, and how was I to know her ache was so large? Why should I accept the ache that stretches from the manicured suburbs of Detroit to my Brooklyn, writhing with ideas? I was writing.

She made accusations about my mental health according to the graduate studies of her firm lady of guidance. These things were similar to what Tommy wanted to say but didn't; it is clear to me now.

The guidebooks say, I am to suffer, and Tommy and Marta believe this too, but it is really so simple. It is all so simple, and here I am pressing center left, with my own will, and I can feel my faint love, my loving place in the world. I can feel my flesh and blood, the center left, my animal heart reviving like a patient now given an antidote. My love will grow immense. It's bigger than two people in my own small life. It is my offering to everyone, to my neighbors on this grey city block and to remote villagers under the hot distant sun. It is my offering to suffering children, the antidote to all.

Acknowledgements

Much gratitude to the editors and publishers of these print publications where individual stories previously appeared:

"Alpha Male." *25 Very Good Stories and 12 Excellent Drawings.* Soft Skull, 2003.

"Intention Neglect." *Thirdest World: Stories by Three Filipino Writers.* Factory School, 2007.

"New." *Union Square Magazine,* November 2010; nominated for a Pushcart Prize.

"The Other Realm." *Columbia Journal,* Fiction Prize Winner and publication, Fall 1998.

"Until It Comes to You." *Bamboo Ridge,* 2006, and *Thirdest World: Stories by Three Filipino Writers,* Factory School, 2007.

Lara wholeheartedly relishes the kindness of her shrewd and charismatic publisher and publicist, Aileen Cassinetto and Michelle Blankenship. You have made this such a high and sweet experience; it is wondrous to be supported in being so freely myself. Dr. Nanette Nacorda Catigbe, our cover artist, you made me gasp. Also, in addition to her Fil-Am community, Lara thanks more good Samaritans on the artistic journey:

Leslie-Ann, Maija, Habiba, Liza and Carl, my brilliant friends, that you believed in me kept me up;

New York City, land of a thousand thousand travelers, land of my birth, thank you for bringing these conjurers to my life;

Also, much appreciation to Angie, aking pinsan, lover of science and tales and sorceress of wika, and our cousin artists and thinkers in Manila, about the islands, and scattered through the Seven Seas. And, of course, more of my family and friends under the endless sky.

About the Author

Photo by Tau Battice

LARA STAPLETON was born and raised in East Lansing, Michigan. Her maternal family is from the Philippines. New York City is her homeland. She is the author of the short story collection, *The Lowest Blue Flame Before Nothing* (Aunt Lute), an Independent Booksellers' Selection, and a Pen Open Book Committee Selection. She edited *The Thirdest World* (Factory School) and co-edited *Juncture* (Soft Skull). Her work has appeared in dozens of periodicals, including *The LA Review of Books*, *Poets and Writers*, *The Brooklyn Rail*, *Ms.*, *Glimmer Train*, and *The Indiana Review*. A writer of prose, poetry, and teleplays, she is developing *1850*. Co-created with Rachel Watanabe-Batton, the television series is set in antebellum New Orleans and is about mixed-race families, taboo and the color line. The project was selected for the IFP No Borders International Co-Production Market. She is also at work on a show about a self-destructive multi-cultural community in Brooklyn and another about a Filipino-American restaurateur with Nicole Ponseca.

She was the recipient of a Ludwig Vogelstein Foundation Grant for Writers and a two-time winner of the University of Michigan's Hopwood Award for Fiction. She was also the winner of the Columbia Journal Fiction Prize. A graduate of NYU's creative writing program, her greatest pride is for her students at Borough of Manhattan Community College of the City University of New York.

CPSIA information can be obtained
at www.ICGtesting.com
Printed in the USA
LVHW021614141021
700428LV00006B/656

9 781734 496550